Mayhem in South China Sea

Mayhem in South China Sea

P.R. Franklin

ZORBA BOOKS

ZORBA BOOKS

Published in India by Zorba Books, 2017

Website: www.zorbabooks.com
Email: info@zorbabooks.com

Copyright © P.R. Franklin

ISBN Print Book - 978-93-86407-42-9

Zorba Books Pvt. Ltd.(opc)
Gurgaon, INDIA

Printed in **Repro Knowledgecast Limited, Thane**

Acknowledgements

First and foremost to my brother, Brig. V.P. Franklin, VSM (Retired), who with his wide reading experience was able to give me critical and unbiased advice on the formulation of chapters to make for better reading.

My thanks are also due to Padma Shri Dr. Prahlada Rama Rao, former Vice Chancellor Defense Institute of Advanced Technology, and former Director of Defense Research and Development Laboratory, for his guidance on the correctness of certain scientific material that I have put out in one of the chapters.

To Rear Admiral Ajit Tiwari of the Indian Navy who after retirement was CMD Hindustan Shipyard Ltd, Managing Director Bengal Shipyard Ltd, and Director Bharati Shipyard Ltd, for his excellent ideas he provided to improve the story.

I am also grateful to my wife, Joya Franklin, for patiently reading the drafts of each chapter and giving me her valuable comments, help in clearing out inconsistencies, loose threads and unnecessary details.

Finally, I am grateful to 'Zorba Books' for publishing this book.

Contents

Prologue

On a calm, sunny, day in early December, Capt. Harry of the Indian Navy had taken off from the naval air station in Arkonam - a naval air base in the coastal strip of the east coast of southern India - with his crew of 7 (including four lady officers) for a sensitive reconnaissance mission over the South China Sea. Heading eastwards to cross the coastline, the utter havoc caused by the cyclone that hit Chennai and its surrounds just a few days earlier, was painfully displaying its tale of miseries on ground that would take months to recover from. Many lives had been lost, hundreds of homes destroyed, and thousands of square kilometers of land inundated by what turned out to be the worst cyclone in a hundred years to hit the Chennai coast of peninsular India.

The P-8i Neptune was a recent acquisition by the Indian Navy from the United States of America. Built on Boeing's 737-800 design and airframe, apart from maritime patrol, it was capable of performing anti-submarine, anti-surface warfare, surveillance, and intelligence gathering mission roles. Additional fuel tanks gave the aircraft a range of up to 2,222km, with four hours on station. Capt. Harry had ensured that these additional tanks were strapped on before take-off, as he might need the extra endurance. He also ensured that the aircraft was fully equipped and armed to meet any eventuality, as per instructions received from 'higher ups'. The P-8i Neptune differed from the P-8 Poseidon built for the US Navy in that it had many pieces of sensitive equipment that were India-specific, and made in India. That gave the aircraft all that was required to perform as an integral part of the Indian Navy, with the required level of discreetness. It also enabled her to communicate through the Indian satellites positioned overhead that were meant exclusively for the Indian Navy's use.

Three major warships of the Indian Navy were, at that very moment, on their way to Japan to participate in bi-lateral naval exercises in the Sea of Japan. Purely as a matter of diplomatic courtesy, New Delhi had informed Beijing about the movement of this Task Group through the South China Sea. The destroyers INS Delhi and INS Mysore, and INS Deepak the Fleet Tanker, having sailed through the Malacca Straits, were about to enter the South China Sea. They were transiting through international waters, along the shipping route, but passing close to some very sensitive and disputed areas of the region. Capt. Harry and his aircraft were being deployed around these ships to reconnoiter the water and air spaces ahead of the formation and ensure their safe passage through these troubled waters. In short, the mission was to provide cover to the Task Group transiting the South China Sea.

As per her flight plan, the P-8i Neptune was to refuel in the naval air station in the Nicobar Islands, catch up with the Task Group and reconnoiter ahead of it, see it through the South China Sea, proceed to refuel in Ninoy Aquino International airport in Manila, and retrace her steps via Changi International airport in Singapore, where she would top up with fuel, and terminate her sortie in the naval air station in the Nicobar Islands.

Flying over the Bay of Bengal during the first leg of her flight plan, the Neptune's crew suddenly detected an electronic transmission in a frequency band used by a certain class of submarines, coming from directly ahead of her flight path.

"*Fish at latitude 9 degrees north*," buzzed the excited voice of the lady operator over the intercom.

The 'contact' had probably just emerged from the Malacca Strait into the Indian Ocean. The crew immediately got to work to analyze it for finger-print confirmation.

"Confirm *it's a submarine. Designated as Contact Alpha*," buzzed the intercom again. It was the High Resolution Imaging

Inverse Synthetic Aperture Radar (ISAR) operator. "*The contact is the wake of a 'feathering' submarine periscope*," he chirped.

"*Confirmed*," added the third crew member after observing the Field of Interest Register (FOIR) onboard. "Contact Alpha classified as *PLA Navy "Yuan" Class conventional diesel-electric submarine, NATO code-name 'Song' Class*," the voice continued.

Having been alerted of the Neptune's presence, the submarine decided to dive deep.

Capt. Harry tried to moderate his excitement and decided to track it for awhile as he had time on hand.

"*Launch Sonobuoys – Pattern Zulu*," ordered Capt Harry.

The Neptune dropped a pattern of acoustic sonobuoys around the last known position of the submarine. Within minutes, the sonobuoys picked up the propeller noise of the submerged submarine and began to relay information to the aircraft. The sonobuoy monitor onboard the aircraft locked on to the dived boat. The signature did correlate to the PLA Navy submarine.

Capt. Harry and his team tracked her for two hours, both with the sonobuoys and the Magnetic Anomaly Detector (MAD) sensor in the tail of the aircraft. She was definitely noisier than both the Indian Navy's Kilo Class and the latest class of indigenously built 'Scorpene' submarines, renamed as the new 'Kalvari' Class. The information gathered would be useful at some future date and augment the data they already had on this Class of Chinese boats.

Capt. Harry recollected the news about eight export versions of this submarine, code-named as the S20 Class, being purchased from the Chinese by the Pakistan Navy at throwaway, 'friendship', prices. '*In all probability, this one was on its way to Karachi*,' surmised Capt Harry.

"*The Submarine captain was either clumsy or had much to learn about evasion*," he mused as he watched the Chinese submarine maneuvering underwater shabbily in a bid to shake off detection.

"*Sonobuoys self-destruct complete*," buzzed the intercom again, after two hours of continuous tracking. The dropped sensors having relayed all the sensitive parameters to the aircraft, the Neptune stopped tracking and resumed course.

Through her indigenous Mobile Satellite System, and her indigenous discreet speech secrecy system, details of the submarine were relayed to the appropriate authorities back home. This would be in addition to the information gathered from the permanently located sea-bed sensors the Indian Navy had laid at the approaches to the Malacca Strait to pick up and monitor underwater platforms entering the Indian Ocean.

Six hours after take-off, and after that little excitement of tracking a submarine, the P-8i Neptune landed in the naval air station in the Nicobar Islands for a fuelling halt. This was pre-arranged and therefore carried out quickly. The additional drop tanks that were empty until now were also topped up. Soon she was airborne, heading in a northeasterly direction, to meet up with the Indian Task Group in the South China Sea.

"*Albatross approaching from westward: Grid reference 848532. Call Sign VWFT. Overhead in ten minutes.*" transmitted Capt. Harry to the Indian Task Group on a discreet radio channel, moments after entering the South China Sea.

The in-flight re-tasking was received from the Operations centre and Neptune was put directly under the operational command of the Senior Officer of the Task Group onboard the INS Delhi, who happened to be an officer with a two-star rank. Rear Admiral Zora Singh, the Task Group Commander, ordered the Neptune to scout ahead of the formation, while maintaining contact with the Task Group on data link all the time.

Normally there would have been no requirement for a maritime reconnaissance aircraft to fly ahead of an Indian Task Group still under cover of own surveillance satellites overhead, and the South China Sea was covered by the Indian surveillance satellites. In this case, however, Capt. Harry and his crew were deployed with the additional task of gathering as much electronic intelligence (ELINT), signal intelligence (SIGINT) and other information as possible, of Chinese activities in the region, using the presence of Indian warships in the area as a cover. The aircraft was well equipped to carry out such roles in peace and hostile conditions. Neptune 20 from the IN320 Squadron got down to her operational tasks, with the specialist lady officers and the rest of the crew members carrying out their duties with trained and practiced efficiency. The plane had her electronic countermeasures equipment, her towed decoy self-protection suite, and infrared countermeasures suite at the ready to cater for all possible eventualities. Taking no chances, Capt. Harry also had his defensive weapon suites made ready for instant use, should the need arise. He was expecting trouble.

Principal Players

Abduweli – A young Uighur, who spent his childhood in his homeland in Xinjiang province watching his near and dear ones eliminated by the Chinese government as part of their efforts to quell repeated Uighur uprisings. Grows up and becomes a separatist.

Abdul Haq al Turkistani – Abduweli's father, who turns into a separatist and enrolls as a member of the *Turkistan Islamic Party*: moves to Pakistan to train separatists to prepare them to come back and fight in his homeland against the Chinese government.

Abdullah Mansoor - A prominent leader of the *Turkistan Islamic Party.* The Party has been formed to free Xinjiang Province of Chinese 'oppression'.

Yusuf – A young Uighur who joins Abduweli to become a separatist.

Ehmet – Another young Uighur who joins Abduweli and Yusuf to become a separatist.

Erkin – The third young Uighur to join Abduweli, but only for awhile.

Jimmy Ahuja – Newly appointed Head of Research and Analysis Wing in the Government of India.

Jack O'Brian – Director of Central Intelligence Agency (CIA), in the USA.

Hafiz Mohammed – A senior member of the *Turkistan Islamic Party,* who plays a pivotal role in this story.

Daura-e-Suffa – A terrorist camp in Pakistan for basic training.

Daura-e-Aam – The Intermediate terrorist training camp in Pakistan.

Daura-e-Khaas – The Advanced terrorist training camp in Pakistan.

ASEAN Community – Comprises of the ASEAN Political Security Community (APSC); the ASEAN Economic Community (AEC); and the ASEAN Socio-Cultural Community (ASCC).

Gamaliel – A member of Israel's secret service – Mossad: posted in their Embassy in New Delhi, India.

Al Turner – A newly appointed CIA agent in the US Embassy in New Delhi, India.

Kaloyanov – A Bulgarian Real Estate builder with a colorful past that keeps catching up with him to satiate his greed for money.

Xin Sheng Zong - The Minister of State Security in the Chinese government.

Yang Zhen - Head of the Counter Intelligence Bureau: a very intelligent man, working under the Minister of State Security.

Ariella and Frieda – Two women Mossad operators, based in Israel.

Captain Grozdan – Master of a Bulgarian merchant ship.

Amram Danielov – The Chief Officer onboard the same Bulgarian ship.

The Seed

The Prime Minister of India had just returned from the 14-days' Climate Summit in Paris, where, among other business, he had 'one-on-one' bi-lateral talks on the side, with six Heads of States present. One of them was with the President of the United States. He had, on his plate, a number of issues to discuss with him, and so had the President of the United States. He was not, however, prepared for one of the points raised on which the President had obviously been well briefed. The Prime Minister listened attentively and did not commit himself in any way. But he promised to do some preliminary work. For a comprehensive brief on the topic, the Prime Minister was asked to 'send someone over' when he got back. Other issues were then discussed. When he got back to New Delhi, he had asked his Office to send him a brief on a certain subject, and mark the file 'For Restricted Eyes'. Three days later, as he walked into his office he found his Principal Secretary waiting for him in the corridor outside his office.

"Come in PS. Have you got what I asked you to bring?" enquired the Prime Minister. "Good morning, Sir. Yes, Sir, I have the file with me" he responded while indicating the file in his hand. He was invited in, and the file with that familiar color denoting that it contained matters of a very sensitive nature, not meant for circulation through normal channels, was placed on the Prime Minister's table.

"Leave it with me. I shall go through it, and if any follow up is required, I shall send for you," replied the Prime Minister. The 'red light' outside his office was switched on to indicate he was not to be disturbed. He then began to read:-

"The South China Sea (SCS) is increasingly becoming an area of hot dispute. Mainland China draws on ancient

historical background, and claims that practically the whole sea belongs to them. They are in the process of drafting a code of conduct to be followed in the SCS, to be discussed with the littoral states sharing the sea with China. The Philippines, Viet Nam, Taiwan, Brunei Darussalam, Cambodia, Lao PDR, Indonesia, Singapore, Thailand and Malaysia, who form the ASEAN, differ in their perceptions. Some of them claim that many of the reefs, atolls, and islands of the Paracel group and the Spratly group have been in their possession and occupation for years. The United Nations Convention on the Law of the Sea gives special rights regarding use of marine resources and exploration, including energy production from water and wind to littoral nations up to 200 nautical miles from their coastline all over the world. When applying these principles in the South China Sea, the picture becomes complex. There are a variety of overlapping claims covering considerable water-space that China finds unacceptable.

It is assessed by some that the South China Sea has around 190 trillion cubic feet of natural gas under it. China sees harnessing this gas a solution to the pollution problem in its country resulting from excessive use of fossil fuel. The United States of America and the rest of the world are of the opinion that the South China Sea should be shared by all for common usage, and that China cannot claim total rights over it. An International Court in The Hague, on an appeal by the Philippines, ruled in 2016 that China has no historic title over the entire South China Sea. It also ruled that China's artificial islands cannot be recognized as islands. China, despite being a signatory to the UN Convention on the Law of the sea, absented itself from the Court and rejected the Court's ruling outright.

Military might and possession being nine tenths of the law, China has seriously embarked on building up military defenses on some of the reefs and atolls, after embarking on massive land reclamation projects on some of them. Also, on the island of Hainan, off the southern coast of her mainland, she has made major investments and built naval facilities to accommodate a large number of ships and submarines. If allowed to continue with these programs, she will most certainly achieve the dominance, control, and exploitation of natural resources she seeks from this region.

Not to be outdone, and determined to give mainland China a run for her money, the ASEAN nations have embarked on a policy of progressively beefing up their military maritime capability as a reaction to Chinese intentions. In recent years these littoral nations have procured some twenty modern conventional submarines from different sources, which are a cause of concern to China. Concurrently, and in a show of solidarity with the other littorals, the US Navy has stepped up its patrolling of these waters with warships, while repeatedly exhorting China to keep the South China Sea as a zone of peace and an area through which peaceful transit by ships of all nations is possible. The US has warned China that any permanent military presence in these waters will only lead to turbulent times in the years to come. The Chinese largely ignore such warnings and continue with their plans for domination of the Sea.

On the diplomatic front, attempts are being made by the rest of the world to dissuade China from pursuing her ambitions of taking strategic control of this sea, and to share it with the rest of the littorals for the benefit of the neighborhood and mankind. This is a slow, ongoing process.

Military build-up in the South China Sea gives China a closer launch platform for forays into the Indian Ocean. Chinese interest in the Indian Ocean Region (IOR) in recent years is well known and quite openly displayed. Her 'String of Pearls' strategy to contain and restrict India in the region is an open secret. She already has a toe-hold in the Pakistan port of Gwadar, and a warship presence off distant Somalia, under the guise of countering piracy. A land route through Pakistan Occupied Kashmir and Pakistan up to Gwadar is under development that will facilitate her using this warm water port *for both commercial and military gains. China is indirectly developing facilities for herself in African countries abutting the Indian Ocean. She is doing the same in Bangladesh, Myanmar, and in Sri Lanka and wooing other littoral states in support of its expanding interests in the region. In the last decade, the Chinese Navy (PLA (N)) has moved away slowly but firmly from a coastal 'brown water' syndrome to an ocean-going 'blue water' image with the acquisition of an aircraft carrier, indigenous modern warships, and submarines, and a massive build program. Their conventional 'Air Independent Propulsion' fitted submarines have been spotted in the Indian Ocean off and on. It is common knowledge that her nuclear powered attack submarines (SSNs) are also making forays far and wide.*

The year 2015 saw mainland China's economic spurt slowing down after a spiraling rise towards the end of the last century and the early part of this century. There are also signs of internal dissent that have been showing up sporadically, like the one against the unpopular government move to suppress Falun Gong. Rallies are being held to protest against the ever growing wealth gap, systematic government corruption, the surge in organized crime, rising unemployment, and environmental deterioration. To add to that, there is the never-ending internal power struggle within the Communist Party that brings the government almost to a standstill every now and then. A bigger problem looms ahead of them; demographically, an ageing Chinese population will struggle with the problem of finding youth to carry forward their futuristic plans in the years ahead. Notwithstanding all this, China harbors grandiose plans of becoming a super power, and is working towards it slowly and steadily, with or without its neighbors' support."

The Prime Minister then went on to read the 'sensitive' portion in the file very carefully. He read the whole brief twice over, and locked the file in his safe. He thought for awhile, and then picked up his secure phone and dialed a number. The person he wanted to reach picked up the phone.

"Good Morning! I want to discuss a matter of sensitive nature with you. Can you come over to my residence at 2300h tonight?"

"Most certainly, Sir! At 2300h; at your residence; tonight. I shall be there. Do I have to bring anything or anyone along with me?" asked the voice at the other end of the phone.

"No!" replied the Prime Minister. "And do not mention this to anyone. Bring no one with you."

No hint on why he was being called was given.

Nurturing the Seed

Jimmy Ahuja settled down in the 'Business Class' seat in Air India Flight AI 121 leaving New Delhi for Washington via Frankfurt. This was a sudden, unplanned, trip for which he was not quite prepared. But in his line of duty, many things did not go according to plan. His predecessor in the chair was suddenly bumped off while on his morning constitutional walk down Aurangzeb Road of Lutyen's Delhi. The news hit the front line of all major dailies in the country, and it was generally agreed that it was the work of Pakistan's intelligence agency – the ISI. The usual charges, denials, counter charges, and counter denials followed. It was then officially put out to the media that he had suffered a massive heart attack and succumbed. What happened did not in any way help to improve relations between the two neighboring countries that have seen four wars since gaining independence more than six decades ago. When Jimmy was nominated as the successor, he had only one request – that his appointment be kept in low profile, and that his family be protected. There he was, in his apartment in Gurgaon when the Prime Minister – no less – had summoned him. The visit was short and brief. "I want you to move into the chair just fallen vacant by the sad and sudden demise of a very capable and efficient man," is what the Prime Minister had said. He was not given a choice. They gave him a bungalow on Safdarjang Lane, opposite the Delhi Gymkhana Club with adequate security arrangements. He quietly moved into his office, off Lodhi Road, in the rank of a Secretary to the government, as the Head of the Research & Analysis Wing (R&AW) of the largest democratic state in the world. The R&AW was India's equivalent of Intelligence Agencies of other nations dealing with matters outside the country. Jimmy answered to the Prime Minister through the Joint Intelligence Committee.

His original ambition was to join the Armed Forces, and with his parents' support and blessings, went through the very rigorous process of selection and entered the portals of the National Defense Academy in Khadakvasla, Pune. He graduated from there, and after another year in the Indian Military Academy in Dehra Dun, joined the Indian Army. He was an exceptionally good officer with above average military traits. Having served well in various Himalayan fronts, he was seconded to the Special Action Group forces for a while and from there picked to join R&AW in their 'China Desk'. In the National Defense Academy, and later in the army, he had picked up Mandarin well and spoke it with some fluency. It went in his favor during the selection process for R&AW. This side-stepping from the main stream cost him his promotion to higher ranks in the army. So he got himself permanently seconded to R&AW from where he prematurely retired at the age of 52 as the Head of the 'China Desk'. That was three years ago. Three years later, he was handpicked by the Prime Minister to take over as Head of the organization he had served these last many years. There was strong dissent shown by members of the Indian Police Service, because they considered it their prerogative to head the organization as a matter of course. One aspirant even resigned in protest. However, their murmurs slowly petered out, as it was no less than the Prime Minister who had personally selected the new appointee.

The reason why he was on the plane bound for Washington was because he was summoned to No.10, Race Course Road, late in the night a few days ago by the Prime Minister who had just returned from the 14-days' Climate Summit in Paris, where a lot of on-the-side unofficial bilateral discussions had taken place between Heads of States. One of these discussions was between the Heads of State of the United States and India, and as one of the follow-ups, someone was to be sent across the Atlantic for a detailed briefing on a very sensitive matter of some urgency and importance. Jimmy recalled the conversation during that meeting.

"I had a discussion on a very sensitive matter with the President of the United States, in Paris. I want you to go and meet the Head of the CIA as early as possible. This is sensitive and to be done quietly. He will be expecting you, so there is no need to make any messages about this visit. I do not want the National Security Advisor to go as that would lead to intrigues and speculations on the part of ever watchful, interested parties. You are new in your chair and lesser known, as of now. That is why I am asking you to go. Listen to whatever they have to say carefully. Do not make any promises. Be noncommittal. When you get back, brief me about the visit," the Prime Minister had stated. It goes without saying that he was not travelling as Jimmy Ahuja, but under a different name. In Washington, he was to meet the Director of Central Intelligence Agency (CIA), Jack O'Brian, in his headquarters in Langley.

Jack O'Brian was made the Director of the Central Intelligence Agency in early March, in the same year that Jimmy had retired from R&AW. As Director, he was responsible for intelligence collection, counterintelligence, interaction with foreign intelligence services, and covert operations, among other things. Before being appointed to the CIA, he had served in the White House for four years as Assistant to the President for Homeland Security and Counterterrorism.

Jimmy mentally went over the file he had read in the short time available to him since meeting the Prime Minister, and his catching the flight. O'Brian had worked with the CIA for twenty five years. His early years in the Agency were spent in the Directorate of Intelligence, looking after the Near East and South Asia. Midway through his tenure, he became the CIA's intelligence briefer to the US President for a spell.

After an assignment in Afghanistan, O'Brian served as Chief of Staff to George Bennet, who was then Director of Central Intelligence. Bennet's retirement saw Jack O'Brien step in as the Center's Interim Director. He retired from the

CIA and worked in the private sector for three years. He was then brought back as the Director of CIA.

Jimmy decided that he and O'Brian had a lot in common, and was looking forward to meeting him. This was a long flight, and another equally long flight awaited him after Frankfurt, where he had to change planes. Before leaving home he had looked with searching eyes at his wife and saw no signs of nervousness or unrest, and that was some reassurance.

"I am required to go out of Delhi on work. I do not know for how long, and you do not need to know where," he said. She nodded her head.

"You are not to breathe a word of this to anyone; not even to our children," he ended.

His two working sons, one in Mumbai and the other in Dubai, were not to be told of this trip. His wife was used to this and accepted it as a part of his job. In her own way, she was a strong woman and a good support for him. Soon sleep overtook him and he turned in, requesting the air-hostess not to disturb him, except for meal servings.

Reality or Fiction?

Jimmy Ahuja checked out of his hotel and arrived at Dulles International Airport to board Air India Flight AI 8644 (operated by Lufthansa) early in the evening – still under an assumed name - for an overnight return flight to Frankfurt. As he slid into his seat, a million thoughts were racing through his mind. His first visit to Langley, Virginia, impressed him. The CIA had just gone in for an organizational change – the first in fifty years – to meet the need to handle terrorism and counter-terrorism. After a courtesy call on Jack O'Brian that extended to well over an hour, it was down to serious business. He found Jack O'Brian an interesting man and someone easy to converse with. He did not appear to be guarded in his conversation, but his words were well chosen.

"Hello Jimmy! – That is your first name, isn't it? I know you have travelled here under an assumed name. Well done! That certainly was desirable. We have some interesting propositions for you and your government. But first, let me give you a run down on what we are doing." He led him to the lounge chairs in the far corner of his room, where, on a coffee table, a laptop was already switched 'on'. Jack was a thorough professional. They were comfortable in each other's company which was why they sat together for an hour. The new organizational changes were explained with the rationale behind what necessitated these changes. A lot more emphasis was being given to terrorist activities in USA and on the global front.

The session over, Jimmy was then taken directly to the East Asia and Pacific Mission Centre, where he was introduced to the Assistant to the Director for Foreign Intelligence Relations, Paul Courtney, and his team of two. "This is Paul, our Director for Foreign Intelligence Relations, and with him are Bob and

Ron from his team. Now, if you will excuse me, I will leave you in their very capable hands for the next session," said Jack, as he shook hands with Jimmy and withdrew with a wave of his hand.

At first these gentlemen were circumspect and watched him keenly while going through the getting-to-know pleasantries over a cup of black coffee that Jimmy detested, but politely sipped. It was only after they were reassured by his positive demeanor that they opened up. They were professional and to the point. The requirement was spelt out to him. Jimmy tried to display no emotions, but what he had heard, shook him up.

"This has the backing of the White House, which is why you have been invited. The very fact that you were cleared to come and meet us should tell you that the proposal has interested your Prime Minister too. We will discreetly assist you with information and resources on an as-required basis, provided the demands are reasonable and justifiable. However, that will only be after we get an assurance that you will be undertaking this task. We will wait for the 'thumbs up' from you after you get back and get your clearance. This operation, if executed, will benefit both our countries. I think our leaders are clear about that. A separate, secure channel of communication will be set up between you and us for this operation." The codes for communications and modus operandi were handed over to him in an ingenious gadget a la James Bond that would not invite attention under scrutiny in normal circumstances. At the press of a hidden button, it could be rendered useless.

"There is one more thing I have been asked to tell you," said Paul before escorting Jimmy out of the building to a waiting car. "Should anything go wrong at any stage, White House – and the CIA – will deny any knowledge of the whole operation or involvement in any form. I hope that is clear." Jimmy had asked for a few elaborations during the session, but was met with dead-pan faces and given none. He tried to compare their set-up with what he had inherited back home. There was no comparison.

A quick glance around told him his co-passengers were genuine travelers – tourists, businessmen, families; nothing to worry about. This was a quick scan he always did and was second nature to him now after years of practice and experience in this profession. He had to meet the Prime Minister on his return and brief him on what had transpired in the CIA Headquarters. The immensity of what lay ahead of him was something he had not expected or ever experienced in his professional life before. This was a humongous task, trustingly put across to him by Jack O'Brian's team in the strictest of confidence. Obviously, the fewer people in the know, the better were the chances of pulling off the operation. That is, of course, only if the Prime Minister agreed to go through with it. Any other Prime Minister would have shrugged it off and diplomatically told the Americans to fight their own battles. However, this Indian Prime Minister was gutsy, bold, and courageous. There was a chance that he would go through with it as it was also in India's national interest. Of course, he too would give it support as long as there were no leaks or compromise of plans. He would also deny all knowledge of it should it come out in the open. Jimmy's head would then be on the block. Of that, he was very sure – and that too so early in his new-found job! Jimmy wondered how the American President and his Prime Minister had got down to this topic in Paris. Was it during their short one-to-one meeting? Surely, it did not come out of the blue; the American President had obviously come briefed and with an agenda. What was the Indian Prime Minister's first reaction? Was he prepared to look at it favorably? Was that why Jimmy was sent off on this mission?

"Excuse me, Sir! Please put your seat-back vertically up. We are about to take off". Jimmy complied with a mumbled apology to the air hostess and went back to the world he was mulling about. All of a sudden he began to feel uncomfortable. Was it his sixth sense telling him there was a pair of eyes boring into him from behind with more than ordinary interest, or was it just his imagination? He decided to wait until take-off to investigate further.

Once in the air and the order to fasten seat belts was relaxed, Jimmy got up and headed for the toilet – the rear one. A casual glance at the passengers showed them all busy with their own preoccupations. He decided to wait outside the toilet at the end of the aisle at a vantage point and watch the passengers from behind. The lighting there was suitably dim and that helped him. He concentrated on the few rows behind his allotted seat and across the aisle. A reasonable duration for use of the toilet had passed, but Jimmy continued to wait. After some more time he saw one of the passengers look back towards the toilet. Their eyes met and the passenger quickly looked away. Jimmy was right. There was someone onboard who was keeping an eye on him. He looked like an American. Was he a CIA agent, or someone else? Jimmy went back to his seat, passing the passenger's seat without even a glance in his direction. The passenger did not look at him either. Once back in his seat, he shut his eyes and pretended to sleep. It was a different matter that sleep would not come to him. After his visit to the CIA Headquarters, he had not slept well last night, and it had nothing to do with the hotel room, the bed, the ambience, or the fact that he was there under an assumed name.

In his early years with R&AW, while on deputation from the army, he had served on the 'China Desk'. Eventually he headed it. Jimmy tried to recollect all that he had worked on then. His memory was sharp and he was able to recall many things that would help him with this assignment, if it was to go through. Naturally, he would have to get an update on what he knew then. He decided to formulate a rough outline plan in his mind and have it ready when and if the Prime Minister asked him how he was going to proceed with the operation. But - where to start? There were many little matters that he would have to study before any plan could be formulated. At the moment he could think of none. He suddenly felt very lonely. He would not be able to discuss this with any of his colleagues in confidence. At least, not for some time: probably never. Mentally, he started listing and prioritizing his courses of actions. He opted out of working on his laptop to avoid attention.

An occasional sweep of his eyes all around showed the 'tail' pretending to be fast asleep in his chair. He was a man of medium height with light brown hair combed neatly with a left parting. He had a sallow complexion and a prominently long and pronounced nose. Jimmy now had a mental picture of him that he could identify fairly easily in a small crowd, if required.

He was interrupted from his reverie by the Air Hostess who served him a sumptuous meal with a winsome smile. The shrimps were particularly well prepared. The meal over, he decided to catch up on sleep. It was a long 8 hours haul to Frankfurt. He would have enough time at the airport lounge to freshen up before boarding the next flight to New Delhi – another 8 hours or so.

The Air India plane glided into Frankfurt airport and landed on schedule. As they disembarked, Jimmy's thoughts went back to the events of the previous evening onboard. The food served to him was of excellent quality and served efficiently. He wondered whether those in Economy Class shared his views. His 'tail' was close at his heels and yet at some distance from him. He noted this and made his way to "A Plus" satellite (T1A) terminal in Area 'A' where his passport was processed. He then moved on to Air India's Executive Class Lounge run by Lufthansa, where he had a wash and breakfast. He made an untraceable call to his wife to check all was well. He did not tell her where he was or that he was on his way back and would see her soon. She did not ask any questions about his return either. Good girl! He had trained her well, and he mentally took all the credit for it. He then moved about in the vast expanse of this large airport to do some shopping for his wife – not that she had asked for anything in particular. She never did. In any case, she did not know where he was going or passing through.

He had enough time to walk around leisurely. His 'tail' did not come to the lounge. Jimmy decided that should he spot him while strolling about, he would walk up to him and exchange pleasantries just to put him in a state of discomfort. No luck. But he was being watched - of that he was sure.

His purchases over, he returned to the lounge to await the announcement of his flight's departure. The announcement would not be heard in the lounge. He would be escorted at the appointed time to his next terminal. A cup of good Indian tea later, he was escorted to the Skyline Train that would take him to his next point of embarkation, to catch Flight AI 120. When Jimmy got there he found his 'tail' there, but ahead of him this time. They settled down in the Business Class section to share the next 8 hours of flying time.

When they landed at Indira Gandhi International Airport at New Delhi, Jimmy took a taxi home. His 'tail' was picked up by a car from the American Embassy with diplomatic number plate 77CD 0138. The car was from the US Embassy. It did not follow his taxi.

A Warm Reception

With the quiet hum of running equipment and the hardly discernible sound of her engines as background noise, the Maritime Neptune aircraft of the Indian Navy, commanded by Captain Harry, went about her task patrolling ahead of the Indian Task Force, in the South China Sea. The Task Force was heading for the Taiwan Strait. Electronic emissions on frequencies normally used by Chinese military equipment were being picked up very clearly by Captain Harry's specialist crew.

"Hello! What is this? This is a new one" exclaimed one of the lady officers to her colleague by her side. The other one responded, "I have got it. It is a new one alright. It's a high frequency, military radar, transmitting from right ahead. They both promptly locked on to it for tracking, analyzing, and recording. "Looks like the transmissions are coming from the direction of Cuarteron Reef," said the former. "That's the new island that now covers about 52 acres after reclamation, isn't it?" enquired the other lady officer. "That's right", said the first one. "It is a part of the Spratly group of islands that has been recently built up and developed by China, to monitor sea and air traffic coming north from the Malacca Straits and other important channels." The crew had done their homework in a thorough manner before commencement of the sortie.

This information was relayed to the Captain who had already received it as part of the intelligence briefing before take-off from Arkonam. As per latest reports, two probable radar towers had been built on the northern portion of the feature, apart from a buried bunker and a light-house. A number of 20-metre long poles had been erected across a large section of the southern portion. The reef also had a helipad, communication equipment, and a pier with a loading crane. Harry quickly turned to the relevant page on his monitor screen to recheck the information he had on the other islands in the neighborhood, as reported by the Indian satellite overhead. "Well done! Keep tracking and recording the transmissions, but look for other electronic emissions also," responded the Captain. The lady officers continued with their tasks in a business-like manner.

The co-pilot, not to be left out of the loop, opened up. "Sir, a little north of Cuarteron Reef is Fiery Cross Reef that has been developed by the Chinese with an airstrip to operate all types of military aircraft, and provide port facilities." Looking at the map on the screen, he continued. "Further to the north east, but a part of the Paracel Islands, is Woody Island that is claimed by both Vietnam and Taiwan, but occupied by China. The Chinese have recently upgraded the operational airfield on the island to accommodate Chinese Shenyang J-11 and Xian JH-7 warplanes. It has aircraft hangars, ammunition storage buildings, two batteries of HQ-9 surface to air missile launch pads for self-defense, and radar stations. We can expect company, if they are alert," he said, looking anxiously at the Captain. The latter nodded his head but did not display any emotion.

Suddenly, the background noise was shattered onboard the Neptune by a radio transmission broadcast on a standard international maritime alert frequency:-

"Unknown aircraft, you have entered Chinese waters. Please change course and get on to the international pre-determined routes. You are now in Chinese air space. Alter Course or you will be challenged."

As there were no ships or aircraft within her detection range, Capt. Harry deduced that this could have possibly come from Cuarteron Reef. He had one of two choices. He could continue with his search and give a reply, keeping his Task Group Commander in the loop, or he could relay the information to the Task Group Commander on the destroyer INS Delhi, and let him reply. A quick reply had to be given since he was under threat of being challenged. Ignoring the Chinese challenge could, perhaps, lead to other serious complications. He opted for the first of his options.

"This is an Indian Naval Reconnaissance aircraft escorting three Indian naval ships on passage from India to Japan. We are in international air space and have the right to innocent passage."

There was silence for awhile. The Task Group Commander onboard INS Delhi, Rear Admiral Zora Singh, who had also intercepted the Chinese message and heard Capt. Harry, sent out a message on the same communications channel.

"This is the Indian Task Group Commander. We have kept your Government informed of this visit and our dates for passing though the South China Sea to and from Japan. Please refer to them for confirmation"

All ships and the Neptune aircraft were in passive electronic warfare mode, giving nothing away, and on the alert for electronic intelligence. All their Electronic Countermeasures gadgets were in a high state of alertness, ready to react to any eventuality. There was plenty of military intelligence coming in and being recorded. Once more, the Chinese signaled:-

"Unknown aircraft, you have entered Chinese air space. Repeat – you have entered Chinese air space. Change course and get on to the international pre-determined routes. You are not welcome in Chinese air space. You are challenging our sovereignty. Alter Course or you will be challenged."

This time Rear Admiral Zora Singh was first off the blocks, and replied:-

"Our position on the chart confirms we are in international waters. Once again, I repeat. Your government is aware that we will be transiting these waters en route to and from Japan. Please check with your authorities to confirm".

The Task Group and the Neptune continued with their original plans and did not alter course. There were no further messages from the Chinese for awhile. Then, the co-pilot broke silence and reported in a sharp voice, "two fast-moving contacts on screen. They are closing in fast." Even as he had finished making his report, Capt. Harry said in a calm voice, "I have them visual. They look like two J-10B medium multi-role combat aircraft." In a tight voice he ordered, "All offensive and defensive systems to State One." This meant that the Neptune was now ready to react instantaneously to any offensive action the two hostile aircraft may make. Both flew over the Task Group before taking up position on either side of Neptune. Capt. Harry could visually sight both pilots in their respective cockpits. He waved out to both of them with a broad, friendly, smile. Each of them then did a 'barrel roll' in an apparent attempt to show Capt. Harry that they were armed. They were armed with PL-10 air-to-air missiles that had a hit range of 20km. Such a display was first put up by them in the much publicized intercept of an US Maritime Reconnaissance plane over the same area, but closer to the Yulin Naval Base in Hainan. That was a few years ago under similar circumstances. The Chinese pilots were signaling him with their hands to alter course and move away in a northerly direction, away from Spratly Islands. Still smiling, nodding his head, and with a thumbs up signal, Capt Harry altered his aircraft gently, in short steps, to the indicated direction. The Neptune had its decoys, jammers, and air-to-air missiles at instant readiness all the while. The Chinese aircraft stayed with him till they were satisfied that he had been steered away sufficiently. They then 'buzzed' the Task Group once again, and headed off towards Fiery Cross Reef in the Spratly Group. Capt. Harry was sure they would come back again, or be replaced by some other form of surveillance. Sure enough, in a short while one of the lady officers manning the radar screen reported, "Radar transmissions from air early-warning ship-borne radar from Bearing 010 degrees, Captain." Captain Harry noted that the emissions were from a warship heading towards them from the Island of Hainan. This was relayed to the Task Group Commander who already had the information gathered by his ships.

This aggressive act, despite New Delhi having informed the Chinese government of the movement of this Task Group to and from Japan, did not augur well towards good Sino-Indian relations. The Task Group Commander signaled this incident to the War Room in New Delhi where a live picture of the Task Group and its immediate surrounds were beamed by the Indian satellite above, and put up on the screen. The Defense Minister was informed, who, in turn, informed the Prime Minister. The Foreign Minister summoned the Chinese Ambassador and officially presented a protest note to him from the Government of India to the Chinese Government. The Task Group continued to be tracked and beamed on the screen in the War Room, in real time.

One of China's modern guided missile destroyers, the Jinan 052C, shadowed the Indian Task Group all the way through the South China Sea, and out of it. This was a definite display of clear intent that ominously signaled to the world that those who would like to exercise the right to 'innocent passage' through the South China Sea, like in any other international waters, would confront the same aggressive posture. The incident caught the attention of world media and showed up the Chinese in poor light.

Unknown to, and undetected by, the Chinese destroyer, an Indian naval nuclear attack submarine, code named 'Black Panther', was in the vicinity, busy tracking and recording her every detail from below the surface of the sea.

ASEAN

Around this time, the group of nations known to the world as ASEAN held a summit meeting in Kuala Lumpur, in Malaysia. In a statement at the end of that meeting, the establishment of the *ASEAN Community* comprising the ASEAN Political Security Community (APSC), the ASEAN Economic Community (AEC), and the ASEAN Socio-Cultural Community (ASCC) was announced. It was the culmination of a five decade long effort of community building since the signing of the Bangkok Declaration. The APSC aims to ensure that countries in the region live at peace with one another and with the world, in a just, democratic, and harmonious environment.

As a follow up to the Summit Meeting, a high level military meeting was scheduled in Singapore by members of the APSC Community. This was in pursuance of their goals for conflict prevention; conflict resolution; post-conflict peace building; and implementing mechanisms. India, Australia, and Japan had also been invited to send their representatives to this Meeting as outsiders, to sit in but not actively participate in the proceedings. The meeting was scheduled behind closed doors. Inviting outside nations selectively did not meet the approval of mainland China, but had the tacit backing of the United States of America. The Chairman, who was from Malaysia, opened the Meeting, and after the normal preliminaries, got straight to the point,

"Members of ASEAN, the main aim of our Meeting today is twofold. Firstly, we have to work towards keeping the approaches to Malacca Strait and the surrounding seas free of piracy. For this, our navies have to work together and make a concerted effort with shared responsibilities. Secondly – and this is a complex one that affects all of us in a more serious way - we need to find a long-term solution for peaceful sharing of the South China Sea, in accordance with the United Nations Convention on the Law of the Sea, through talks and diplomacy. We need to have unity in purpose and present a united front with a common aim when we talk to others outside our group, as the South China Sea is as precious to us as it is to our common adversary. I propose that we devote the first day to the first subject, and the next two days on the second subject. At the end of three days, if anything positive comes out of this Meeting, we will share our findings and proposals with China, the United States of America, and the UN as ASEAN's suggestions and recommendations towards peace in the region."

Also, at the same time, in *RSS Panglima* (Naval Training Base) located inside Changi Naval Base in Singapore, a secret Meeting was scheduled between senior submarine operators of the navies of Singapore, Viet Nam, Malaysia, Indonesia, and Taiwan who operate their submarines in the South China Sea. Outside invitees to this meeting were a senior officer each from the Indian and Japanese navies' submarine service, as it was general knowledge that these two countries also deployed their submarines in these waters. No US Navy representative was invited for this first session as they operate and deploy nuclear submarines in consonance with their own global interests. It was decided that a decision to include them in discussions at a future date would be considered later.

Singapore being the host nation, the Meeting was chaired by the officer commanding "RS Challenger – Submarine Training Centre." In his opening address, the Chairman drew the attention of other members to a few vital issues.

"We welcome our honored guests from other navies, and officers from the Singapore Navy, here present. In the last few years, we have seen that the number of navies operating submarines in our waters has increased steadily. Also, the number of submarines operating in our waters has also progressively increased. A few years from now, with steadily increasing number of submarines within the same boundaries of water, we are likely to step on each others' toes with disastrous consequences. We have dense shipping lanes and lots of shallow seas that limit the possibilities of two or more submarines operating in such areas. There are many impediments. There is the risk of underwater collision, and submarines colliding with deep draught merchant ships. There are static seabed installations like oil rigs. There are innumerable fishing vessels. This Meeting is being held in furtherance of the aims laid down by the APSC, to work out a cohesive method of operating each nation's submarines without mutual interference, and for sharing the intelligence so gained by each of us amongst ourselves, so that the water space of the South China Sea can be mapped." He paused for the interpreters to do their bit, and then went on.

"The PLA (Navy) has facilities in Yulin Naval Base, on the southern coast of the island of Hainan. The base can support and operate up to twenty nuclear, and an unspecified number of conventional powered submarines in the South China Sea, in the Pacific Ocean, and in the Indian Ocean. That is why our governments have spent unaffordable sums of money to build up our respective submarine fleets. We need to keep an eye on the activities of the PLA (Navy) and their ships and submarines, on a routine basis." This time he paused for effect, and looked at the front row of naval personnel from neighboring, littoral countries. The interpreters done with this bit, he continued, "A combined methodology of planned deployment and information sharing would be an economical one, and avoid duplication of effort. Such a system was practiced by both NATO and WARSAW navies in the Baltic, The Black Sea, the North Sea, the Mediterranean Sea and the Eastern shores of the Atlantic before the Cold War ended and the Soviet Union broke up. We may like to consider a similar, workable solution for the South China Sea that would benefit ASEAN." He stepped down

With such a two-pronged approach, ASEAN seriously went about the business of finding a solution to the two major problems confronting them. Both Meetings turned out to be beneficial to all present. A number of options were considered, and recommendations made. They even arrived at the modus operandi to be adopted, in broad terms, under various conditions and situations in so far as operating submarines was concerned. It only remained for them to translate their decisions into detailed planning and actual execution on ground.

Towards the end of the session in *RSS Panglima*, the Indian Naval officer, of the rank of Commodore, requested that he be given an opportunity to speak, which was acceded to.

"Gentlemen, with due apologies to our Japanese representative present here, I have been authorized to offer you ASEAN members a special piece of equipment that can be installed on any or all of your submarines with ease, should you want it. This equipment helps submarines operating in the vicinity to monitor each other discreetly up to very great ranges, particularly in tropical waters."

"Are you referring to the underwater telephone?" asked the Chairman.

"No, it isn't an underwater telephone, Sir, but something that is far more effective and not detectable by those without it. The equipment has been designed and manufactured in-house by the Indian Defense Research and Development Organization, and installed on Indian submarines, where they are working well during conduct of coordinated submarine operations. There is no need to dock the submarine for installation, or pierce the pressure hull," continued the officer

"At this stage I am not permitted to say anything more, but if your navies are interested, then please make a formal request, in writing, to our Ministry of Defense, and its acquisition will be progressed expeditiously," said the Indian Navy Commodore.

The meeting was then concluded. All navies professed an interest in this equipment, and resolved to pursue the matter.

The Moment of Truth

The Prime Minister of India was an exceptionally busy man and worked with whirlwind fury and endless stamina, like a man possessed. His daily work schedule began even while others were lolling about in their beds, and went on till late hours in the night. Every day: every week: every month. He did not believe in holidays. He wooed the major powers of the world and invited them to invest in India, make in India, and in the process make India self reliant. The nation was fortunate to have him leading the country at this stage when the world was just recovering from a terrible recession. He was honest and sincere, and had great ambitions for the Indian nation and its people. Already, the countries' GDP growth rate had overtaken that of China, to become the highest growth rate in the world. His main disadvantage was his team – a group of typical run-of-the-mill politicians who were not a patch on him as far as honesty, efficiency, and dedication went. They did not work at the same speed and sincerity. He had to get work out of this motley crowd, much to his frustration.

The earliest that Jimmy Ahuja could arrange for an audience with him was during the week following his return from Washington. He requested for a one-on-one meeting after sunset, and got it. It was unscheduled. He was very conscious of the fact that the lesser the people who got to know about the project, the more its chances of going through to its logical conclusion. It would be safer for him too. He considered the pros and cons of roping in the National Security Advisor from the Prime Minister's Office into this limited circle of people who will be in the know. He had nothing against the individual although the latter was one of the many from the Police Force who had tried to dissuade the PM from appointing Jimmy as

Head of R&AW. That was purely on professional and 'empire-building' grounds and not because the NSA had anything personal against Jimmy. Jimmy decide that it was best that he be kept out of the loop, and requested the PM not to have him present for at least this first briefing. After that, it would be the PM's prerogative to rope in or keep out whoever he chose to. It was arranged that Jimmy see the Prime Minister alone.

The meeting took place at the appointed time. Jimmy began with a quick background briefing, while conscious of the fact that much of what he was about to say would probably be what the American President and the Prime Minister of India had discussed during their last meeting in France. The PM listened to him patiently. Then he gave a detailed briefing on what had transpired in the CIA Headquarters at Langley, Washington. Once again, he was given a patient hearing with only raised eyebrows and occasional frowns coming now and then from the man he was briefing.

At the end of the briefing, the PM sat pensively for a long time, mulling over what he had been told, and even beyond that, thought Jimmy, as he watched him silently from where he was sitting opposite him.

At last the PM glanced at him and asked, "Do you think it can be done without the operations being traced to either of our two countries? If discovered it could lead to great embarrassment and consequences to both nations. I do not want even a hint of suspicion to fall on either country. Do you understand? Give this careful thought and remember my caveat. If you cannot fulfill these conditions, we can go back and tell them, and drop the whole business. Give it some thought and see if you can find a way of going about it. If it is successful, the whole Asia-Pacific Region will benefit, and so shall our country. When will you be ready to give a presentation on how this is going to be executed? Remember what I said, and I am repeating it once again. I do not want India's name dragged into this at any stage before, during, or after the operation, whether a success or a failure."

Jimmy said he would need a month to work on it and be ready with an answer. The PM agreed to give him that one month. The meeting was then over. No notes, no recordings (?), and no witnesses were there to share what had transpired.

Just as he took permission to leave, Jimmy remembered that he had omitted one matter.

"Sir, I forgot to mention one little matter; on my return flight, I was tailed all the way from Washington's Dulles airport to Frankfurt and from there to Delhi by a rep almost surely from the CIA. He chose not to recognize me or engage me in conversation. At Indira Gandhi International Airport, he was picked up by a car from the American Embassy." The PM thoughtfully nodded his head and saw him to the door.

Jimmy took a circuitous route to his house and headed home after ensuring that he was not being tailed. Brooding and lost in thought, he realized he had a lot of work ahead. This was one operation in which he could not directly involve his subordinates. He would have to get them to work on inputs for him without giving away anything. Indians would not be visibly involved in this operation. This he would have to ensure. At this stage, he had no idea about how he was going to get the job done, despite the many hours he had spent in mulling over it.

His wife greeted him with "Dinner is ready. I have had mine and am now going to watch the Pakistani serial on 'ZEE Zindagi' TV Channel. You will have to eat alone." Jimmy nodded his head and headed for the dining room. His wife did not want to know anything about what had transpired.

The Uighur of Xinjiang

In another part of the world, in a remote and backward part of China far removed from the eastern prosperous belt that is shown to the world as the symbol of a modern, rising, progressive nation, the Chinese Government was wrestling with a situation that had been brewing for well nigh seventy years. They were approaching this problem in a slow and deliberate manner, hoping to find a solution with minimum fuss and publicity. This is in China's north-western land-locked region, in the Province of Xinjiang.

'Xinjiang', in Mandarin means 'New Frontier'. The present region came to China as late as during the Qing Dynasty, in the 19th Century. The Province of Xinjiang had been under Chinese care as a Protectorate off and on, in one form or the other, from as early as 60BC when the Han dynasty ruled China. Its population till about 1000AD largely comprised of a mix of people from what is now Iran, and Indo-European Tocharian peoples. Later, with the invasion by Turkish Muslims, the Uighur tribe became the predominant people of the region. Xinjiang passed through various hands; sometimes with Russia; sometimes with the Chinese; sometimes under no one. After annexation in 1949, Xinjiang became an autonomous Province of China, and the Uighur became Chinese citizens. Since then, over the years, there have been numerous tussles between the Uighur and the Chinese, with the former wanting to be independent of the latter.

Geographically, the Province is subdivided into two distinct areas - the Dzungaria with the provincial capital, Urumqi, in the north, and the Tarim Basin, in the south. Across the border, to the west of the Xinjiang Province is Kirgizstan; Kazakhstan lies to its north-west; Tibet borders it in the south.

Unlike other nomadic tribes of Central Asia, the Uighur of Xinjiang led an urban lifestyle in spaced out towns along and across the ancient Silk Route from China to Europe. They were spread out all across the Province of Xinjiang and lived together with a sprinkle of Han Chinese who was locally present. Most Uighur followed a form of Islam that has emerged from Sufism with its original roots in Persia (Iran). The Han Chinese practiced a form of Chinese Buddhism that evolved from the original religion influenced by Confucianism and Taoism. In recent times, the resettlement plans of modern China had seen an influx and flooding of Han Chinese- now mostly Communists - into the Province, and they now formed more than fifty percent of the total population. Han had usurped power and suppressed the Uighur, making them second class citizens in what they traditionally considered as their land, leaving them dissatisfied and causing many of them to flee or to relocate. Then there were the Hui Muslims. They practiced a different variation of the Islamic religion to the one practiced by the Uighur. They are an ethnic group of Chinese who are spread all over China. They are also present in Xinjiang. As they are ethnically close to the Han, they invariably got preferential treatment over the Uighur. Most of the Uighur had therefore moved away and congregated largely in the southern Tarim Basin. A few Uighur still lived in their original towns and cities up north. In the capital of the Province, Urumqi, those remaining were mostly now not-so-wealthy pavement shop-keepers and traders. Some have fled the region altogether, and the population of Uighur in Xinjiang, from a position of dominance, is around a mere lowly fifteen percent.

The religion of the Uighur promotes and encourages tolerance, peace and peaceful co-existence. Yet, the Uighur of today are an unhappy or dissatisfied lot, and far from peaceful or tolerant. The reasons are many. They are not happy with the Chinese presence overshadowing them in such large numbers in a land they once dominated; they do not like suppression of their religious practices (they have even been given a list of Uighur names of Muslim origin that have been banned by the Chinese government. Consequently those holding those names have had to change them and ensure that their children are not given those names else they would be denied education in schools); many Uighur have now become separatists; Hui Muslims being shown preferential treatment over the Uighur community has further irked them; there is infighting within the Uighur community, and so on. As a result, there have been many clashes over the years between the Uighur and the government authorities – some even violent and harsh. Some of the Uighur have turned active mercenaries, dissidents, separatists or rebels – call them what you will - and are a constant thorn in China's side. Others have fled the country they love so much. Some train abroad, and come back to hurt the very land of their birth, even while their kith and kin are residing there. From this lot emerged a group of young Uighur, whose future would be linked with Jimmy Ahuja's interests, as events unfold.

The Groundwork

Sitting in his office in Lodhi Estate, a few days after his meeting the Prime Minister, Jimmy was going through routine matters he dealt with every morning - looking at urgent telegrams and messages, reading through important matters his Heads of Departments had put for his perusal, looking at his appointments for the day, the Meetings he had to attend, so on and so forth.

Today's main bit of information was about the explosions that had taken place in Brussels airport the previous day, and in a subway station in central Brussels. The same terrorists involved in the Paris terrorist attacks were apparently involved here also. He quickly scanned the report submitted to him and his eyes paused to read the next bit more deliberately. Secretly recorded videos of the movements of a top Belgian nuclear scientist were recovered from the house of one of the suspects involved in both the Paris and Belgian attacks. What were these for, wondered Jimmy? Were they planning to kidnap him or entice him into doing something for them under duress? What could they get out of him?

Since his morning "IN" tray was full, he dismissed the Belgian incident for the moment, reminding himself to get back to it after the routine work had been completed. Here was another one of some interest; a French journalist under disguise had made contact with someone in Bulgaria and managed to get an abandoned Soviet origin nuclear warhead from him. For what purpose?! The report did not say.

There was an intelligence report on the Chinese attack on Indian troops in the Ladakh region of Kashmir that had resulted in many casualties on both sides. The Chinese were building their China Pakistan Economic Corridor (CPEC) road to Pakistan through Pakistan Occupied Kashmir and this had been objected to at the highest level by India. Without warning, Chinese troops had crossed the Line of Control from Skardu and had carried out an unprovoked attack on Indian troops. They had met with stiff resistance and a cease-fire was agreed upon before further escalation could take place. This report would have to be analyzed and put up to the Joint Intelligence Committee, and Jimmy made his notation on the file.

There were some more details about Pakistan's many terrorists training camps, and these could go into the jigsaw puzzle picture being compiled by R&AW, for the government to use to political advantage at an appropriate time.

There were routine reports from some of their many moles placed all over the world in strategically located places. Some were their own agents; some were double agents. Nothing of particular interest! All normal!

Jimmy heaved a sigh of relief when he had emptied the "IN' tray and filled up the "OUT" tray. He rang the bell for the peon to clear the tray. He called for the Joint Secretary Area II who covers China and South Asia. Mr. Sant Singh appeared in moments, and Jimmy asked him to sit down, and offered him a cup of tea that was in keeping with traditions of Indian government offices. The peon brought it in moments, as if by magic, and withdrew.

"What is your latest take on the Island of Hainan?" Jimmy asked Sant Singh. This was in continuation to previous discussions they had had on the South China Sea and the disquiet in that region.

Drawing a notepad out from his pocket, and leafing through the pages, Sant Singh answered, "Sir, from my sources, I gather that tourism has been hit because of water problems on the Island. People living there have stopped drinking local tap water for many months because the water is polluted with heavy metals. A Company – Sanya Yacheng Water Supply Ltd – the main supplier of water to the touristic city of Sanya is unable to supply potable water and tourism is suffering. The Songtao

Reservoir in central Hainan, so important for irrigation, has seen dead fish floating up by the hundreds last month. Drinking water is now being arranged from the mainland. The Chinese government is working towards a long-term solution to solve the problem. I also got some initial information about the Chinese planning to make three or four floating nuclear power stations so that they can park them in the Spratly and Paracel Islands and Reefs that they are developing, to provide uninterrupted power to the facilities coming up there. I presume desalination plants will follow. I will do some more work on this and give you more details, Sir."

"That's a new one!" mumbled Jimmy, "There aren't any floating nuclear power stations anywhere else in the world. They sure think out of the box. I wonder if they will succeed."

"Apart from the usual media reports that everyone, including me, have read, do you have any inside information on what the Americans and the Philippine government are planning in the region to counter Chinese efforts to set up strategic posts?" asked Jimmy, looking into his junior colleagues eyes intently.

"I have nothing of interest on that score yet, Sir. The new Philippines government in power is making overtures towards China that is upsetting the United States of America no end. An American under-water drone has been seized by Chinese naval ships just off Subic Bay, quite close to Philippine waters. In the western portion of the South China Sea, ASEAN are planning some sort of coordinated maritime deployments to track Chinese ships and nuclear submarines emerging from their underground hideouts in the island of Hainan. To what purpose, I cannot say at this stage; they have kept the Americans out of their plans for the moment, and that is interesting; probably not to irritate the Chinese. Perhaps we can get something on that from our Director, Naval Intelligence. The Navy had sent officers to attend the meeting on the subject held in Singapore recently. I shall come back to you with more on that" Sant Singh offered.

The recently concluded ASEAN Political Security Committee Meeting was then discussed for awhile. When Sant Singh had drained his cup of tea, Jimmy dismissed him with a curt smile and then pensively gazed out of his window.

As soon as his subordinate left, Jimmy switched on the 'red' light to indicate to visitors that he was not to be disturbed, and slipped out of his back door. There was one "entry" door to his room, but two "exit" doors, of which one was regularly used. He took the second one to his car and drove away by himself to India International Centre on Max Mueller Marg, where he had an appointment with someone. This was a meeting that he had worked out with a certain person on a regular, and yet irregular, basis, in different places across New Delhi. He was on time.

As he parked, got out of the car, and crossed the courtyard, Gamaliel slipped out of the shadows and came up to meet him with a warm shake of his hand. He was of medium height but muscular and well built. He always wore a genial smile that endeared him to anyone and everyone who conversed with him. Behind his mask of geniality was a very shrewd and intelligent brain that worked over time.

"Good Morning! We are safe here. No one is interested in us, or at least it appears so." He said with that famous genial smile. They headed for the cafeteria and ordered a cup of black coffee and tea. An Israeli citizen, Gamaliel was located in New Delhi and was from Mossad – an organization that was created by Israel way back in 1949, and now considered as the third or fourth top intelligence agencies in the world. They dealt with intelligence compilation, counter terrorism, and conducted secret operations, concentrating mainly on Arab nations.

R&AW and Mossad had a good relationship with each other, and often came to each other's aid in a big way when warranted. As is customary between friendly intelligence agencies, they 'cautiously' shared trivial bits of information that were apparently of no great importance but, nevertheless, pieces that went into a jigsaw puzzle towards eventual compilation of a larger complete picture. Jimmy was sorely tempted to tell Gamaliel all about his American visit and lean on this burly man's experience for advice, but decided against it. They talked of piracy, terrorism, Syria, Turkey, Russia, Ukraine, Pakistan, Iran, China, the insurgency from Pakistan into India near Pathankot in Punjab that resulted in a failed attack to destroy warplanes, the Uri attack that followed, and so on.

"I cannot understand why you are reluctant to cross the border and give them a resounding beating every time they do this. You have the capability. We do it in Israel all the time, and it keeps our opponents quiet for awhile. The one and only 'surgical strike' that your army carried out recently should have been followed up with more to fend off offensives from across your border," said Gamaliel.

Jimmy smiled and replied, "Military capability must be exploited with political will", and left it at that. Coffee and tea over, they got up, shook hands, and departed down separate corridors.

At the main portico, Jimmy passed a man who looked familiar to him. He was looking away. He couldn't, however, recollect his name immediately, or where he had met him, if at all. The India International Centre held many conventions, attended by prominent Indians and members of the diplomatic community. He got into his car and drove back to his office. Halfway down, it suddenly hit him. He was the same American who had 'tailed' him on the flight back from Washington after his visit to the CIA headquarters – the one with a long nose and left hair parting. Warning bells started ringing in Jimmy's head. Did he see who Jimmy had been with? He decided he must pursue this matter further.

He was back in his office after a lapse of two hours, and continued with his daily office chores. He called for his Joint Secretary Area IV, who looked after the Americas.

Jimmy gave him the date that he had travelled back from Washington and said, "Find out from the passenger manifest list of Air India as to who were the Americans who travelled from Washington to India via Frankfurt in 'Business Class'."

He did not give any reason for asking for this information. He did not divulge that he was also on the same flight, as he had travelled under an assumed name. No one from his office knew about his trip. No one needed to know anything about his visit – at this stage. But sooner or later, he would need help as he couldn't go to the Prime Minister with a plan with only him as the actor - like some sort of Indian James Bond.

The Joint Secretary did not show any curiosity. He was used to being told only what he was expected to know and no more. "I'll get back to you with this information, Sir" he said, and with that he was dismissed.

Abduweli

He was of average height and good build. His muscular frame showed the fruits of regular handling of weights. His rough, large, hands were that of a person who had used them for extreme physical work. His short brownish-black hair was neatly combed, and his clean-shaven countenance gave the impression of a person who was tidy in his habits despite a hard life. His ever-searching intelligent eyes were grayish-blue, stretched between a tight skin and barely visible, giving nothing away. His face and sharp prominent jaw-line portrayed an air of quiet determination that could turn to harsh cruelty when required. His well washed clothes were that of any youth making do on a limited budget. A checked shirt carelessly tucked into a pair of well worn denim jeans, held together by a broad leather belt with a prominent buckle, gave him an air of confidence. A pair of sneakers completed it all. He answered to the name Abduweli.

Although young in years – he was a little over 25 – Abduweli had already lived through what most in other parts of the world would take half a century to experience. A central Asian of Turkish origin, he was born in Kashgar city in the province of Xinjiang in the northwestern part of China, into a Uighur family. He grew up in what could be termed as troubled times for his tribe as they were in confrontation with the Chinese government to whom, the province belonged.

Abdul Haq al Turkistani, his father, had also grown up in these parts under the same prevailing conditions of turbulence and oppression – ever since the Chinese annexed their province in 1949. Even the autonomous status the Chinese government bestowed on their Province in 1955 did not satisfy the Uighur people. At the age of 30, handsome Abdul Haq al Turkistani married a young, pretty, 20 year-old, light grey-eyed Uighur woman of Turkish origin – Meryem – who came from a respected and known family. She was very pretty. He used to lovingly call her 'Meryemgul', the suffix 'gul' meaning 'flower'. Meryem bore him four children in all. Abduweli was the first to be born within a year of their getting married. Two sisters followed him, and then a brother. Young Abduweli formed a part of the second generation of Uighur living through that long period of dissidence and unrest in post 1949 Chinese province of Xinjiang.

During one of the many incidents of violence, uprisings, and quellings by the authorities, Abduweli lost his mother, his two sisters, and his baby brother to a hail of bullets. There was an uprising in the town of Kashgar located in the south-western part of the Province, and the Chinese government used force to put it down. There was bloodshed. He was a witness to the carnage that saw scores of people – his people – dying. At that time he could not understand what was happening. He was only five years old. In the years that followed, he could not forget the pain, the screams, the blood, and the look of terror in the eyes of those running helter-skelter that he saw from his shelter behind a refuse bin across the road from his home that day. The loss of his mother and siblings – all of them on that one fateful day - was even more painful. Only he and his father were left in the family after that blood-bath.

His father was heart-broken and enraged. One day, he called his son and seating him on his lap said,

"Son, Abba has some work to do that will take me far away for a long time. I am going to leave you with your Aunt Patigul for some time, till I return. You remember Aunt Patigul? She came last year and stayed with us for a week? She lives in the next town not far away. She is a kind person and will look after you well; she will feed you, give you new clothes to wear, toys to play with, and she will send you to school where you will learn great things."

"But Abba, I want to stay with you. I don't want to go away from you" replied Abduweli, clutching his father, and tears started building up inside him. He was upset. His father hugged him tightly and whispered in his ear,

"Son, I love you very much, but I have some very important work to do. Some day you will understand this. Right now, do as I say and wait for me to come back. Tomorrow, I shall take you with me to Aunt Patigul's place. While I am away, I will be happy to know you are safe and sound."

His father knew he was making the right decision because in his new role he would be travelling far and wide and would not have time to look after his son. Little Abduweli was moved to his aunt's house in Korla City in Bayingolin, on the south-eastern border of the Province. It was a small town, nestled between the Tianshan mountain range in the north and the Kunlun mountain range in the south. The latter marked the border between Xinjiang and Tibet.

Abdul Haq al Turkistani, join the Uighur separatist movement *Turkistan Islamic Party,* to take on the 'oppressive' Chinese Government. He soon found himself in Waziristan in Pakistan, training to be a soldier to fight the Chinese oppressors.

In the prevailing conditions that he grew up in, Abduweli had no real childhood – no friends, no fun, and none of those carefree moments that childhood offers, and was his by right. He was clandestinely employed in child labor in the courtyard of the *madrasah* to produce illegal weapons and ammunition required by the Uighur movement against their Chinese oppressors. In the *madrasah*, he was taught the Koran and how to read and write in Pashtu and in Mandarin. The meager sum of money he brought by way of wages was handed over to his aunt and was barely sufficient for him not to be ousted from her home. He was fed, and he had a place to sleep; for that he was grateful. His aunt had no children; they were also killed during an earlier raid by the government authorities in a bid to put down the religious leanings of the Uighur. Affection was not something that his aunt was wont to part with, as that emotion had dried up long ago. So he received none. He often reminisced about his mother and his siblings, but only for short durations as scenes from the horrific carnage would soon follow, and re-open old wounds.

In the early part of this century, one of the assaults led by Pakistan forces on an Al Qaeda camp in Waziristan, saw the death of one of the prominent leaders of Uighur rebels, who was training recruits in one of the terrorist camps there. Abduweli's father, Abdul Haq al Turkistani, was in Waziristan at that time. Having completed his training, he was retained as an instructor for other younger aspirants. He was promoted and asked to take over the late leader's mantle and operate from Waziristan - a mountainous region in West Pakistan, on the Afghanistan border. Two years later, he rose to a prominent position in Al Qaeda's Central Committee – *Shura Majlis*. So he was now a man of substance in his new-found role.

The years passed. Through overheard bits and pieces of conversation in and around the *madrasah* back home, young Abduweli gathered that his father had moved to Pakistan; or was it Afghanistan? He only had a vague idea of where these places were located- again gathered through pieces of idle, whispered, conversation in his place of work. His father was now supposed to be an important person. There was no communication from his father, which was something he rued.

Then, a few years later, the local radio announced that a prominent leader of a Chinese terrorist group, who was serving on Al Qaeda's top council, may have been killed in an airstrike in Pakistan's Taliban-controlled tribal agency of North Waziristan. The report was not confirmed. That day, while he was working in the *madrasah*, one of the others there approached him and said,

"Abduweli, have you heard? Someone from our tribe was killed in an airstrike in some place near where your father is working. I heard it on the radio this morning. I hope it is not your father."

Abduweli was very upset to hear this. One Abdullah Mansoor, a prominent leader from the *Turkistan Islamic Party,* was in the neighboring city of Hetian, in Xinjiang, at that very moment. Abduweli caught a bus and rushed to that city. After a lot of running, searching, pushing and shoving, Abduweli managed to get an audience with him. "*Assalam Alaikum wa Rahmatullah wa Barakatuh,*" greeted Abduweli. He went on, "I, Abduweli, am the son of Abdul Haq al Turkistani, and have come to see you from Korla City in Bayingolin. In Korla City, there is a rumor that my father, Abdul Haq, may have been killed somewhere in Waziristan in Pakistan or Afghanistan. Please tell me this is not true. Where exactly is my father? How can I get in touch with him?"

Abdullah Mansoor raised one hand in a sign of greeting and replied, "*Alaikum Assalam wa Rahmatullah.* So! You are Abdul Haq's son?" He looked him up and down approvingly and continued, "Yes, I know your father. He is doing some wonderful work in support of our movement in the place where he is working. He is much respected there and his name and fame has spread far and near. You say he died? Who told you that?"

"Sir, the people back home say there was an American air attack on or around Waziristan and my father may have been one of the victims."

"But I have not heard any such thing," interjected Abdullah Mansoor, which gave Abduweli a thin ray of hope.

"How can I see him?" asked the young man, and got an immediate response, "By enrolling yourself in the *Turkistan Islamic Party* and going to where your father is, for training. Are you willing?"

Abduweli's response was not long in coming. A feeling of rage and the urge to hit out at all those who hurt the Uighur people overwhelmed Abduweli. He resolved to join the forces engaged in the Uighur liberation struggle. He was over 25 years of age now and very fit.

"Yes! I would like to join immediately. Please send me for training to where my father is operating" was his quick response.

Uighur with separatist tendencies, or wanting to join terrorist groups to carry out acts of aggression against Chinese authority, follow a well-beaten surreptitious trail that takes them from Xinjiang to South East Asia, and then on to Turkey. Turkish embassies in these countries help them. In Turkey, their forged passports are confiscated and they are then given genuine, valid, Turkish passports which enable them to move about freely, travel to Pakistan for undergoing training in their terrorist camps, or to join the ISIS in any part of the world after the training. There was a shorter route and that was the road built between Kashgar in Xinjiang and Islamabad in Pakistan through the Karakoram Pass in the Himalayas, but Uighur were not allowed to take this route to Pakistan, by the Chinese.

Abduweli was enrolled into the *Turkistan Islamic Party* and soon on his way to Pakistan via the well-beaten circuitous route. He wanted to train well and hit the Chinese where it hurt them most. Revenge! That was all he was looking for now. There were no hugs; no tearful farewells. He even imagined, for a moment, that there was a look of relief in his aunt's eyes as he took leave.

Eureka!!

On his constitutional early morning walk in Lodhi Gardens, located equidistantly from his office and his residence, Jimmy Ahuja's mind went back to issues discussed in Langley some weeks ago. No, 'they' had not contacted him and neither had he contacted 'them'. He had to present a plan to his Prime Minister first, and this was no matter to be dealt with in a hurry. Time was available and was not a criterion for executing the task. Yet Jimmy found that he could not take his mind away from this operation. Even while dealing with other official routine matters, he found himself going back to this issue whenever he could take a break from his other work. Jimmy accepted this as one of those things that happen when you have no one else to share and discuss the subject with. Therefore the responsibility for its success or failure would depend entirely on him. That is, if the Prime Minister gave the green signal.

This morning, he led his thoughts in a new direction. How would other countries or organizations deal with this? What line of action are they likely to adopt? The Europeans and the Africans would not be interested in such an operation. The Russians looked at the target nation as their ally and would also not be interested. His mind focused on the US of A. They were obviously interested. They had vast resources at their disposal and more than one option available to achieve their aim. They must have mulled over it, but after careful consideration hit upon the idea of using India as a tool for achieving their ends. No responsibility could be pinned on them; they could deny they were ever involved; the enemy's-enemy-is-your-friend principle can be exploited; India had the capability to do it; the success of the operation would benefit them and their allies in the region. Fire the gun from someone else's shoulder! They had been following such a line for decades and with all their allies, with their own self-interest paramount.

He thought of Pakistan. They were training and using terrorists against India and constantly creating problems across the border, using methods that were affordable, affective, and yet falling short of open hostilities. They were helping the Taliban in Afghanistan. They had both State sponsored terrorists and non-state sponsored terrorists working for them. In Jimmy's opinion, they were doing it well, much to India's irritation. However, he was sure this would be short-lived as the negative aspects were already hitting back at them. The terrorists were creating havoc in Pakistan itself, and getting out of their government's control. More lives were now being lost to terrorists in Pakistan than in India. He recalled the attack on their military school, and the attack on their police academy.

Terrorists! Why not get terrorists to do the job for him? He recalled the newspaper headlines of a few days ago that read "Bombs tear through Belgium's international airport and a subway station in central Brussels." The terrorists involved in the Paris bombing were believed to be involved in this one too. A tingling sensation ran right through his body! Yes! This was a possible solution Jimmy was seeking all these days. The more he thought about it, the more he liked the idea. India's name could be kept out of the operation, and the terrorists could take the credit, if one could call it that. If they were *jihadis,* they wouldn't mind laying down their lives in the process. Even *fidayeens* could do the work.

Suddenly, while lost in deep thought, his way was blocked by a person in jogging suit. "Namaste, Jimmy *Sahib*! I have been trying to catch your eye during every round of the Gardens we have been taking. Either you have pretended not to notice me, or are genuinely lost in deep thought. Which is it? This is the third time we are passing each other. Are you angry with me? All well? Is anything bothering you?"

Jimmy's thoughts were now interrupted and he found himself face to face with the Cabinet Secretary who also walked daily in Lodhi Gardens. In fact, many senior government officials used the place for their morning and evening constitutional walks, and security in and around the Gardens were always very tight.

Jimmy mumbled a hasty apology and decided to talk to him for a moment to avoid any misunderstandings.

"Morning Sir! I am so sorry. I was not looking at who was, and who was not, walking in the Gardens today, and was immersed in my own thoughts. Nothing serious! Just being my usual self!" he said jovially, to laugh it off.

"What's the thinking in North Block, Sir? Do you think the ruling *Bharatiya Janata Party* (BJP) will win the elections in Uttar Pradesh and the North Eastern States and form a government with a majority in all of them?" he asked of the Cabinet Secretary.

"That would depend on what sort of inputs the Intelligence Bureau fed the ruling BJP government, leading to the campaign tactics they eventually adopted, wouldn't it?" countered the Cabinet Secretary, with a mischievous smile.

"Fortunately, Sir, my work does not include internal intelligence. The trouble is one cannot fathom what goes on in these politicians' minds. One minute they are at daggers at each other, and in the next minute they are hugging, and backslapping each other like long lost friends. Do you feel the Yadavs war will be their downfall? What is your take?" countered Jimmy.

There was no answer. The Cabinet Secretary chose to avoid giving an answer. After a few more pleasantries they nodded their heads and parted company with a wave of hands, going in opposite directions so that each could get back to their own thoughts.

Yes! Terrorists! - But which ones? – And from where? More importantly, how could he get them to do the job? Here was a whole new field of thought open to Jimmy to consider. If he couldn't work out something plausible, he would have to think of something else. Suddenly, an idea came to Jimmy's mind! It just might work, but he would need some help to see it through, and he knew who all to ask. His mind began working on this idea more and more, as he thought of the many channels that were available to the R&AW to get in touch with these sorts of 'contacts'. He singled out one of R&AW's 'moles' he had worked with in the past, and resolved to contact him. It took him awhile, but he found the mole in Istanbul and gave him some work to start the ball rolling. This man was capable and had proved his worth in the past. He would, however, need time to work things out. Jimmy suddenly felt confident and began hoping the Prime Minister would accept his plans. If the 'go-ahead' is not given to him, he could always call up his contact and cancel his instructions.

Later that week he had been invited to a cocktail party in the US Embassy, in honor of the visiting US Secretary of State, who was going on to officially visit The Peoples Republic of China from New Delhi, after three days of hectic consultations in the Indian Capital. Jimmy had accepted the invitation as a matter of routine. Normally, he disliked going to these official functions, but it was a part of his job. Now, with his brain working overtime, he thought it would be a useful function to attend.

The Separatist's Route

Abduweli crossed over to Bangkok after a long and arduous journey that took him across the southern border of China into Myanmar, then on to Laos, through Cambodia, and into Thailand. There, according to the instructions he had received, he was to lay low and rest for awhile before moving on. A short halt was planned during which the Turkish embassy would prepare their papers for onward travel. He was not alone. With him were three others from the Uighur tribe who came from other towns in the *Junggar Basin*. They were strangers, but with the same aim – to train and fight against the injustice meted out to their clan by the Chinese government. They met up in Cambodia and slowly got to know each other as they travelled to Thailand together.

Erkin was the tallest of them all, who was twenty one years old and hailed from the capital, *Urumqi*. He was a light-hearted fellow who did not appear to take anything seriously, and was always on the lookout for some fun. However, unknown to the others, behind that devil-may-care attitude was an excellent ability to think and reason logically when required, backed by nerves of steel. It was good to have him as a part of the group.

"My whole family is dependent on one income. I have six siblings. My father owns a pavement shop and does not make enough to meet the very basic needs of the family. They wanted me, as the eldest, to find work and augment my father's income. I thought it would be better if they had one mouth less to feed! I told them that I was going to the nearby town of *Wujiaqu*, looking for a job. I did not go back. I decided to join the *Turkistan Islamic Party*. I was given some money for this journey, and here I am!" was his short introduction to the others.

The curious one was Yusuf. He was always asking questions, whether intelligent, relevant, or not. He was twenty four years old and had spent all his childhood in the city of *Turpan*. His entire family was repeatedly harassed because of their religious faith, and finally exterminated by the Chinese soldiers in one swoop of *Turpan,* six months ago. Like Abduweli, he was a lone survivor from that carnage. Bitter and angry, he wanted to take revenge, and enrolled in the *Turkistan Islamic Party*. Like the others, he too was on his way to be trained as a separatist.

Ehmet was an intelligent, smart, twenty four year old Uighur from a very large family in the border town of *Kumul* in Xinjiang Province. He was fed up with the harassment of Uighur people by the government. Unable to study any further than middle school because opportunities were constantly being denied to them as a tribe, and favor repeatedly shown to the Han and the Hui, Ehmet also joined the separatist movement. He met up with the other three in Cambodia and accompanied them up to Bangkok. All four decided they would travel and stay together all the way up to Turkey.

On the northern part of *Rattanakosin*, near *Khao San Road* and in the downtown district of *Banglamphu* in Bangkok, Abduweli and the others found food and shelter. Abduweli was briefed about this shelter before leaving Xinjiang, and again in Cambodia. A local Thai, who was the conduit to and from the Turkish embassy; who spoke his language; had been housing transiting Uighur rebels at his residence for years, and arranging for their onward journey, was their contact man. Here, at his place, they could maintain a low profile and move about without drawing attention. No one in this downtown part of Bangkok asked questions because no one wanted to know anything more than their own business. Curiosity in this area only led one to trouble.

Abduweli was low on finances, and asked his host, "I am running out of money and need some to last me till Turkey. I am prepared to work for it. Is there any way I can earn some?" He knew that in Turkey he would be replenished, or so he was told, with enough to last till commencement of training in Pakistan.

"You are not supposed to be inordinately visible in these parts, so if you are thinking of a regular job, forget it!" said his host, but continued, "Let me see if I can find something for you that will not get me or you into trouble."

Bangkok, the capital of Thailand, has a charm of its own that attracts tourists throughout the year from all over the world. Apart from her unique palaces and heritage monuments of Buddhist culture found everywhere, her friendly people give visitors a very relaxed atmosphere to bask in, and have a peaceful sojourn. Many outsiders come on intended short visits but stay on for a number of months; some even for years. The four of them stepped out to see the lie of the land in a country that was so different to theirs. They were warned by their local Thai host not to get into any conversation or brawls with the locals. In a few hours they returned, totally overwhelmed by all that they had seen.

It was the month of September. It was time for the annual *Chak Phra* festival of *Wat Nangchi* on the *Thonburi* or west side of the river in Bangkok. It is held in September every year. It commences with a small boat procession, which grows as more boats join on the way. The bigger boats carry reliquaries – relics of saints – onboard. The water-borne procession then spends the rest of the day in a quiet portion of the river with some of them participating in races before passing through the *Khlong Bangkok Noi* canal and back to the monastery from where it all originates. The boat owners who participate in races call for volunteers to row these very long snake-like boats, and pay them handsomely. Spectators bet on these boats heavily, and so a lot of money is involved. Abduweli, a temporary resident in Bangkok, had the necessary physique to fulfill boat owners' requirements. His host walked into his quarters one evening and announced,

"I have got a job for you. You have to be a part of a rowing boat that will participate in the races a few days from now. I told the owner you have the physique and stamina to row well. You won't have to talk at all as I told him you are dumb. He has asked you to be at his place for practice starting tomorrow morning," said his host.

A delighted Abduweli attended all the practice sessions. He learned quickly and rowed powerfully. His team practiced hard for many days, but could not win the prized trophy. Nevertheless, he was paid well for his contribution and effort.

After the race and the ensuing celebrations, Abduweli got paid and returned to his 'digs' to find a visitor waiting for him – a visitor who was a complete stranger to him, but from his part of the world. What followed next charged and excited him no end. This was just what he was looking for. This was what he needed at this stage.

The Presentation

When Jimmy drove into the Prime Minister's residence on a Sunday evening, exactly one month after that first one-to-one briefing he had given him, he wasn't surprised to see the National Security Adviser (NSA) already there. They smiled and shook hands, but did not say a word to each other while they waited for the Prime Minster to appear. One of the staff appeared and ushered them into a sound-proofed room further inside the residence where they found the leader of the largest democracy in the world waiting for them. He folded his hands in the traditional Indian way, and greeted them, and they reciprocated.

"Ahuja *sahib*, I have asked the NSA to be present to hear what you have to say. We are both ready to listen to you now. So please sit on the sofa across us and tell us all, at your own speed, and in your own style. Be comfortable. Relax! We will not interrupt your trend of thoughts, and will ask questions, if any, only after you have finished". He glanced pointedly at the NSA when he said this. "This room is suitably protected from eaves-droppers. Please switch off your mobiles and communication and recording devices. Nothing said in this room will be taken out in any form except in your minds," he remarked with a hint of a smile. Then the Secretary Research and Analysis Wing began his presentation.

He described the Chinese version of ownership of the South China Sea, as they saw it. He then went on to give the versions of each of the other nations who had a stake in the region. He rattled off figures on tonnage of international shipping that passed through the area; of the amount of hidden and as yet untapped quantities of undersea oil and gas believed to be available; and international opinion on the use of the South

China Sea. He highlighted the clauses from the 1982 United Nations Convention on the Law of the Sea (UNCLOS) that was applicable world-wide. He reminded the Prime Minister of India's commitment to help the Vietnamese government with offshore oil and gas exploration in the region despite Chinese disapproval. He also mentioned in passing how ASEAN was looking towards India for any and every form of help in the dispute with the Chinese on the South China Sea.

Jimmy then went on to specifics on maritime matters in the region. He highlighted all activities that the Chinese were conducting both in the Paracel and the Spratly groups of reefs and atolls that included fishing, land reclamation, construction of airfields, jetties, berthing facilities, installation of electronic surveillance systems, positioning of warplanes, and construction of buildings on reclaimed land. He also narrated what Vietnam was doing on the reefs in their possession.

"All the Chinese creations," he went on, "are logistically and militarily supported by bases on the southern maritime coast of China, and from the island of Hainan. They are now studying the possibilities of stationing floating nuclear power plants off these atolls and reefs to supply uninterrupted power."

Jimmy then described the military facilities being set up in Yulin naval base, in the touristic island of Hainan. By tunneling inside the hillside to house up to twenty nuclear weapons armed submarines, and creating berthing facilities outside for up to six aircraft carriers, destroyers, and other naval craft over the next few decades, China was proceeding with the four-fold intention of controlling the South China Sea in totality, supporting the facilities in and around the reefs, harvesting marine food and all the natural gas and oil in the region, and making her entry into the Indian Ocean that much easier. He elaborated on Chinese submarine ventures into the Indian Ocean. In the not too distant future she would become a reckoning force at India's doorstep with the help of the facilities in the South China Sea, and the 'String of Pearls' she was building around our subcontinent. He did not fail to mention the China-Pakistan Economic Corridor up to the port of Gwadar through the Karakoram Pass, Pakistan Occupied Kashmir, and the length of Pakistan, that the Chinese were building.

"For the benefit of the NSA, may I repeat what transpired in CIA Headquarters, Sir?" Jimmy enquired of the Prime Minister. He got an assenting nod and repeated all that he had told the Prime Minister a month ago.

"And now for the plan I have conceived," he went on. He paused for a moment and found renewed interest in their eyes. He continued. They listened. Without going into any nitty-gritty, he outlined a fairly comprehensive plan – the result of hours of thought with many sleepless nights, years of military training, extensive research work, and days of weighing pros and cons. At the end he assured them that, neither India nor the originator of this whole scheme would be suspected or apportioned any blame before, during, or after its execution. If the plan succeeded, a severe temporary set-back to Chinese dominance of the South China Sea, and plans for exploitation of the Indian Ocean, would follow. This would give India and the US of A some time to work out plans to neutralize Chinese ventures in the region. If it failed, nothing would be lost.

There was a momentary silence, and then the barrage of questions followed – mostly from the National Security Advisor. Jimmy answered all of them with a frank "Yes", "No", "Might be", "Point taken", "I will work on that", "Will be careful", "Cannot give you an accurate answer at this stage", "Too early to say as yet," " I have the necessary contacts", etc, etc.

At the end, the Prime Minister got up and led Jimmy to the door, while signaling the National Security Advisor to stay back. "Don't do anything till you hear from me," he said. Jimmy drove home confident that his candid approach went down well with his two-man audience. From the type of questions thrown at him he felt they had bought, or will buy, his idea, and that he better get down to the matter in hand in real earnest. Every minute detail will now have to be worked and re-worked on; checked and rechecked; and guaranteed the highest probability of success.

When he got home, his wife opened the door to find her husband looking relaxed and cheerful after many days. "What's for dinner? I'm ravenous."

"Dinner is on the table. I have had mine and am now going to watch the Pakistani serial on 'ZEE Zindagi' TV Channel. You will have to eat alone." He resignedly headed for the dining room. He definitely did not approve of his wife's interest in Pakistani TV serials that she religiously watched every evening, but did not demur as he had not provided her with alternate forms of entertainment and distractions.

Jimmy was shaving in the morning after his normal walk in Lodhi Road Gardens a few days later, when he got a call from the National Security Advisor on the classified phone line to say that the Prime Minister had cleared his plan, and from here on he was on his own. He was once again reminded that the Prime Minister, the Indian Government, and the National Security Advisor, had no knowledge about this matter at all. The phone went dead. There was no time-frame or date by which the operation should be executed. He stared into the mirror at himself, and suddenly, for a fleeting moment, felt all alone in this world. He was 'on'!

Gamaliel

Gamaliel was born in Haifa of Jewish parents who had emigrated from Bulgaria to Israel to participate in the nation-building program of the 'promised land' in 1948. That was the year Israel was given nation statehood. His parents still had a link with their motherland through their siblings who chose to stay back and live under the mantle of communist rule because there was too much to walk away from. He often fondly recalled his visits to Bulgaria with his parents during his formative years. The whole country was greener than Israel, he would complain every time they came back. Like every fit and able Jew, he began his compulsory military service at the age of eighteen. That service was of thirty month's duration for men, and twenty months for women. After completing compulsory military service, he worked in a kibbutz for a few years, turning up annually for an 'update' military course of a month's duration to keep him abreast of the latest developments in weapons and weapons systems. All citizens went through this, and kept their personal weapons and battle equipment in their respective homes. In this way, in event of war, seventy eight percent of the armed forces could be mobilized in about eighteen hours. He got married and settled down to a routine life as a family man. After awhile, work got dreary for Gamaliel, and he left the kibbutz to join the officer cadre of the regular army. He rose to the equivalent rank of Colonel before he branched out to join Israel's secret service – Mossad.

The Mossad had a unique way of operating compared to intelligence organizations of other nations. Instead of having a large net-worked force, it tapped the large number of loyal Jews from communities worldwide, through a unique system of '*sayanim*' (Hebrew for volunteer helpers). Consequently, it normally had less than fifty officers deployed as '*katsas*' (field intelligence officers), all over the world. A '*katsa*' is the equivalent of a 'case officer' in the CIA. The motto of Mossad is: "By way of deception, thou shalt do war". Gamaliel was good at his work and therefore assigned to India as a *katsa*. He was a good man. He had a few skeletons in his cupboard from his bachelor days that he carefully concealed. That apart, once he got married, he sobered down and lived a chaste life.

Mossad also had women on their roles. Women agents were all very intelligent, good looking, and often called upon to use their looks, figures, and feminine wiles to achieve the objectives set out by the State for them. In certain situations, they were more advantageous to be utilized than men. They could flirt in dangerous conditions to extract favors and information. Flirting was fair game. However, Mossad drew the line short of getting them to sleep with their 'victims'. Mossad had had many successes in the past with this line of approach. All their women agents were very well trained, fighting-fit, and excellent soldiers. They were also capable of taking care of themselves. They were generally unmarried, as the work was considered to be too demanding for women with families. Women were deployed to hunt in pairs.

India was an important nation as far as Israel was concerned. Heading eastwards from Israel, after crossing the Islamic states of Jordan, Saudi Arabia, Iraq, Persian Gulf nations, Iran, Afghanistan and Pakistan, the first non-Islamic nation was India. India just had to be an ally, and Israel would go to all sorts of lengths to be there for India whenever needed. Israel had permeated every Indian government office on matters considered to be important to Israel's national interests, and continues to do so. Placing Gamaliel in India came out of that strategy. India would help Israel one day against the Islamic world when the need arises, was the latter's firm belief. Like his predecessors in New Delhi, Gamaliel had many reliable contacts in India at all levels. Keeping in touch with Jimmy Ahuja with periodic regularity was an essential part of his work. He had done the same with Jimmy's predecessor who, unfortunately, was bumped off by the Pakistani ISI. It was Israel who first forewarned the Indian government about an impending attack on the Indian Intelligence agencies. The warning went unheeded as the Indian parliamentarians were preoccupied with state elections at that time.

Gamaliel found Jimmy Ahuja to be an intelligent and shrewd man, and one with whom he could work pleasantly. During their last meeting in the India International Centre, he sensed that there was something Jimmy wanted to share with him, but did not. He decided to let Jimmy come out with it – if at all – in his own time. Their next meeting was next month in the Taj Palace Hotel, on Sardar Patel Marg, in a privately booked room under a false name.

Gamaliel also discovered that it was quite easy to interact with members of the diplomatic corps of other countries here in New Delhi, without eyebrows being raised. The Delhi Golf Course was one example of a place where diplomats of different countries could be seen in twosomes, threesomes, or foursomes, driving, pitching, chipping and putting in a very friendly and cordial atmosphere with gay abandon. The India International Center was another place where one could hold a quiet discourse over a cup of tea. The 'Pragati Maidan', or the Exhibition Grounds, was yet another place for interactions while walking through the many exhibiting stalls. The Indian Intelligence agencies generally left the diplomatic corps alone unless they had specific reasons to follow them around. However, they did keep a watchful eye on all Embassies and High Commissions – the majority of them being concentrated and located in Chanakyapuri. That was Gamaliel's opinion. His CIA counterpart had also the same opinion – the earlier one. A new CIA agent had just been posted into the American Embassy, and Gamaliel was yet to meet him. He decided he would give him time to settle down before getting acquainted.

Having spent a little over three years in India, he had grown to love the country and its people, and had made many genuine friends in social circles, both in and out of the ambit of his profession. It was a very diverse country indeed, with so many languages and different cultures. Keeping them together as a nation and providing all that was expected by the common man was a herculean task, he conceded. He admired the present man in the Prime Minister's chair, who was making a genuine effort to speed up the clock of progress in an otherwise laid back and complicated country. He wished him well. His time in India was coming to a close, and he expected to be transferred in the near future, perhaps back to Israel for awhile and then on to another country. He knew that breaking up with this country and walking away would be painful for him and his family. The warmth and friendship of India was already flowing in his veins. Some things just had to be expected and accepted.

Hunting with the Hounds

In a portion of the South China Sea, far beneath the stillness of the surface waters disturbed now and again by the wakes of fishing trawlers, with or without heavy nets, was a black, menacing, steel leviathan, moving with impudence and freely patrolling the sensitive waters shared by many littoral countries. The Black Panther was steering a south easterly course out of the Gulf of Tonkin, and heading into the more open waters of the South China Sea. If she continued on this heading she would pass the Paracel group of reefs and atolls on her port, and a little later, the Spratly group of reefs and atolls on her starboard side. She was on a free patrol by herself, armed with a war outfit of tube-launched land-attack missiles of Indian origin, Russian origin torpedoes, and four lethal underwater remotely controlled autonomous drones also of Russian origin. The torpedoes were similar to the ones in the possession of the Chinese navy. Her underwater detection sensors told her she was not alone. Dived as she was at a safe depth, she was tracking some sixty contacts on the surface all around, at a safe distance from her. Most of them were either Vietnamese fishing trawlers that were now astern of her, or Chinese trawlers mostly on her port side. They were a perpetual menace with their trawls and nets spread out and every care had to be taken to avoid their fishing areas. Her sonar screen also showed eight merchantmen plying on the shipping route between the Malacca and Taiwan Straits. She would term such a situation in the South China Sea as 'Ops Normal'. They could all be watched and tracked but were of no threat or interest to her. This was the normal traffic in these waters.

The Captain had received 'intelligence' about a PLA (Navy) nuclear submarine that was preparing to slip out of its hillside tunneled shelter in Hainan Island's Yulin naval base, under cover of darkness. This was why he ordered a south westerly course to steer from their position the previous night. The report, when decrypted, read:

"From: SDHQ. To: Black Panther. One pumpkin for home delivery tomorrow or the day after; Intimate firm delivery schedule"

The word 'pumpkin' stood for a 'boomer' or a strategic, nuclear propelled, submarine; 'home delivery' meant it was heading for the Indian Ocean; asking for 'firm delivery' meant it was to be tracked and details reported. Hidden from spying eyes, the vast cavern, dug inside the hill next to the tourist city of Sanya, was capable of housing up to twenty nuclear submarines. Satellite tracking of these submarines was difficult as they dived inside the cavern and left harbor, submerged. Around the tunneled entrance were jetties and piers to accommodate aircraft carriers, destroyers, and amphibious assault ships. In the approaches to this naval base, the Chinese had positioned boom nets and moored sensors to detect and monitor intruders spying around in the vicinity. The Black Panther was aware of these and had an accurate 'fix' of where they were located. She also knew which portions of these defenses were vulnerable and could be penetrated, after careful observation over a period of months. However, she was not heading that way today. She wanted to locate and track the Indian Ocean bound submarine from somewhere around the Spratly group to identify her selected transit route for entry into the Indian Ocean, and report her movements more accurately to higher operational authorities. Looking for a submarine in mid-ocean was like looking for a needle in a haystack, but the Black Panther had Indian designed sensors ideally suited for early detection at long ranges in tropical waters, and this was one big advantage she had over other submarines with their sonar sensors designed and built in northern, temperate, climes for operating in those waters.

"Captain, Sir! Control Room: Submarine on our starboard bow, classified as a Malaysian 'Scorpene' Class conventional boat. She compares well with the fingerprints we have in our data bank and appears to be the one going by the name of *Tunku Abdul Rehman*. She is steering a southerly course, and is unaware of our presence," reported the Officer of the Watch after collating information from the Sonar Operator.

"Assign her a track number and watch her. Officer of the Watch! Take suitable precautions and don't let her detect our presence. We do not want to mess around with her or let her know we are around," said Captain Sharma, Black Panther's Commanding Officer, from his cabin. It was normally acknowledged that diesel-electric conventional submarines were slower but quieter than nuclear power driven boats. But the Black Panther was of a superior fifth generation design, and could hold her own against her conventional counterparts.

"Aye, Aye, Sir!" responded the Officer in the Control Room, while ordering the boat to assume ultra-quiet state.

Later that afternoon Captain Sharma received another report from the Control Room.

"Captain, Sir! Control Room: there is a submarine on our starboard bow. She appears to be the *Swordsman,* a conventional 'Archer' class boat of the Singapore navy. The Malaysian *Tunku Abdul Rehman* is on our starboard quarter, and appears to be sending a message to the *Swordsman* using similar equipment to what we use between our submarines. Both are being tracked and appear to be unaware of our presence as we are outside the range of their detectors."

Captain Sharma smiled. So! ASEAN submarines were now using the equipment India had sold them after the last ASEAN meeting. This was good news indeed! The South China Sea would now be monitored in a more organized manner to make tracking of Chinese submarines that much easier.

"Log their messages, but keep distance and do not let them be aware of our presence" repeated the Captain to the Officer of the Watch in the Control Room. He then wended his way into the Control Room to see things for himself.

It was about sunset time when the Sonar Room reported detecting a destroyer of the PLA Navy coming up from the Black Panther's port quarter. She was at some distance, well beyond periscope visual range.

"Classify her! Do not give me vague reports. Come on Sonar Operator, wake up!" The Captain showed some annoyance that was observed by all in the Control Room. This was surprising because they knew him to be a man who usually portrayed only steely emotions while onboard. He, however, had his reasons. He wanted to get on with the business of getting the complete underwater picture without delay.

After awhile the classification report came in. She was a Type 052D destroyer; one of the *Luyang III Class,* the first of which was rolled out just five years ago. She was a state-of-the-art, very modern, destroyer, comparable with the best of her type in the world. The Captain paused to reflect; these destroyers were sometimes used to provide cover to strategic submarines entering or leaving harbor, or as escorts for a good part of their path in sensitive or restricted waters. Sometimes strategic submarines were also escorted by another submarine of the SSN variety. Captain Sharma was well aware of their tactics, which were evolved from Russian tactics. Having trained in Russia, and having operated in these waters for many years onboard three different types of submarines, he found the Chinese tactics very much the same. Nevertheless, prudence dictated that he be careful, and not jump to any conclusions.

The Black Panther was now equidistant and abeam of the Spratly islands on the port side, and the Vietnamese coastline on the starboard side. The Captain altered her course to south-south-east, dived deeper, and increased speed, to get her clear of the shipping lanes between Singapore and Taiwan. Once clear, the SSN turned around to face the Spratly islands and virtually came to a halt, lying in wait – waiting to pick up the first sounds of the destroyer, or the ballistic missiles carrying submarine, and even, possibly, of an escorting Chinese SSN. The Malaysian *Tunku Abdul Rehman* was being tracked on her port quarter. The latter was at the mouth of the Gulf of Thailand. The Singaporean *Swordsman* was almost astern of the Black Panther, at some distance. This was good, thought Captain Sharma. The more distractions around for the Chinese submarine, the better it was for the Black Panther. The Chinese submarine would keep busy; that is, if she, or the destroyer above, or the other SSN, detected any of them. It also helped that at this time there were six merchant ships in the vicinity, on their shipping routes, moving to and from the Malacca Strait.

The propeller noise of the destroyer was first picked up right ahead. It was coming closer. It was lost temporarily when the Black Panther increased speed and dived deeper to cross the shipping lane, and passed two merchantmen, both oblivious of her presence. All eyes and ears in the Sonar Room were straining to get the first emissions from a submarine expected to be in the vicinity of the destroyer. The destroyer would undoubtedly be the noisier of the two and would drown emission signals from the submarine, which was the aim of providing her as an escort. The strategic submarine would be moving under the destroyer or a little astern of her at the same speed, to make it difficult for anyone to pick her up. The Black Panther continued to wait at creep speed, covering very little distance, and making minimal noise. She had stopped her main propeller and was now propelling with her side thrusters that made confusing muffled and indistinct noise. She moved at right angles and away from the path of the approaching destroyer to open lateral distance and then turned around and waited again.

"Captain, Sir! *Tunku Abdul Rehman* has just sent another message to *Swordsman*. We have logged the message. The former appears to have locked on to the destroyer," reported the Officer of the Watch. The Captain did not acknowledge, but mentally ticked it off. It is possible that the former had indeed detected the Chinese destroyer's presence and was alerting the latter to take over tracking. While that was fine, it was important that the Black Panther not be discovered.

"Control Room, this is Sonar Room: faint submarine propeller noise picked up ahead of the destroyer, both heading in the same direction". That was it! The Captain was exultant! He was anticipating this and he was proved right. There *was* an SSN ahead of the SSBN and the destroyer above. The Black Panther remained still. She was sufficiently far away and noiseless to be safe from detection. What seemed like eternity was only about an hour; the Chinese formation went along the shipping route, past the Black Panther, and opened out in range, on her port quarter. All she had to do was to now wait for the destroyer to break away to return. She maneuvered to face the receding formation, and slowly tailed them.

Captain Sharma was thinking overtime. Nuclear submarines generally avoided the Malacca Strait and entered the Indian Ocean through the deeper Sunda Strait between the Indonesian Islands of Sumatra and Java, or through the also deep Lombok Strait near Bali, remaining submerged throughout. Which route will the Chinese submarine follow this time? No doubt the SSN will escort the SSBN into the Indian Ocean. The Black Panther would track these two after the destroyer left them, to find the answer.

At 5 degrees north Latitude, just short of Laut Island belonging to Indonesia, the destroyer turned around and retraced her path along the neutral shipping route, and headed back to where she had come from. The Black Panther side-stepped her and now increased speed to continue tracking the SSBN. It was easy to make her out as every now and then the Chinese SSBN would do a fish-tail maneuver to check if there was anybody on her tail. This was anticipated and the Black Panther remained some distance away, out of her reduced listening range astern.

The SSBN selected the Sunda Strait and headed for it. The Black Panther turned around to return to her waiting station, her present task done. She would transmit this information at the earliest opportunity to the authorities in the Andaman & Nicobar Islands. The Chinese SSBN would have an 'Indian reception' awaiting her once she entered the Indian Ocean, and would be tracked relentlessly thereafter by both the Indian and American forces in the region. The two countries shared information on Chinese forces operating there, on a regular basis.

Hafiz Mohammed

Sitting on a bench across the road and opposite to Abduweli's accommodation on *Khao San Road*, Hafiz Mohammed, was waiting for the young Uighur to turn up, for he had important work with him. A middle-aged man who always referred to himself as a man from East Turkestan, which is an alternative and original name coined by the Uighur for the province of Xinjiang, he sported a clean cut beard supported by a mop of curly hair on his head with the central portion bald and devoid of any growth. The bald patch could be seen by those around only when he bent his head downwards, or by those taller than his six feet in stature. He was fair skinned with very alert and lively grayish blue eyes, but the premature weather-beaten lines beginning to show on his face betrayed the tough climatic conditions he had spent his youthful years in. He was very intelligent, had a quiet disposition, and a well built muscular frame. He refused to refer to the Xinjiang province by its Chinese name. He had not resigned to accepting the fact that his beloved province now came under Chinese government control. A series of tragedies and events in his life led him to join the *Turkistan Islamic Party*. This party had allied with the *Islamic Movement of Uzbekistan*, and from that day onwards sent its field members to train in Pakistan along with the *Tehreek i Taliban Pakistan*, and *Al Qaeda*. He was also trained there.

After successfully completing his very rigorous training in Pakistan, and on his very first mission in Afghanistan, he got a hip injury and lost his agility. This led senior party members to utilize his services in locating and recruiting new members into its fold. In this new role, he operated from Pakistan and Turkey but travelled far and wide, across many countries that included France, Belgium, United Kingdom, Iraq, Syria,

Afghanistan, Lebanon, Egypt, Libya, Cambodia, Thailand, Indonesia, and even as far south as Australia. Over the past few years he had built up a very effective world-wide intelligence network stretching from Australia and Indonesia in the Far East, to France, UK, and Belgium in Europe, for locating and recruiting potential volunteers to join the *Islamic State of Iraq and al-Sham* (ISIS). It was on one such recruiting mission that he had now come to Bangkok. Among others, he had set his eyes on Abduweli of whom he came to know through Abdullah Mansoor from Xinjiang. This was the same Mansoor whom Abduweli had met to inquire about his father in *Hetian* in Xinjiang a few months earlier, and who had recruited him into the *Turkish Islamic Party*. He needed Abduweli for a special mission that had come up recently.

Hafiz arrived in Bangkok during the annual *Chak Phra* festival of *Wat Nangchi* when all eyes were on the festivities at hand, and he could move about unobtrusively. He found his way down familiar streets from earlier visits, to *Rattanakosin* to where Abduweli was residing, only to find him not at home.

"You have a person by the name of Abduweli staying with you. I want to speak with him." The statement of fact was followed by a request in an authoritative tone that sounded more like an order than a request. The landlord did not take it amiss; he had met Hafiz on earlier occasions also, and was familiar with his brusque way of speaking.

"He is not here now. He is participating in the festival race. He is a strong fellow. I have placed a bet on the boat he is rowing in." replied the landlord. Hafiz frowned. Recruits were always told to lie low and avoid getting into the limelight.

"May I wait for him in your place?" asked Hafiz of the landlord, but in a more humble way this time. A nod in the affirmative gave him license to enter the house and sit down. No questions were asked and no explanations given. The landlord offered him a bowl of '*johk*' (rice porridge), which he politely refused as he had just eaten.

After a long wait during which he managed to even have a nap, the man he was looking for had still not arrived. The sun was setting and he decided to step out, cross the road, and take in some fresh air. He must have been sitting there for some half hour when he saw a Uighur approaching from the western end of the road. He entered the house Hafiz was keeping an eye on. Giving him a minute, Hafiz crossed the road and entered the house to find the young man engaged in conversation with the landlord. Seeing him, the landlord abruptly left, leaving young Abduweli facing Hafiz. They sized each other up and down, one suspiciously and the other appraisingly, until the stranger spoke.

"Looks like Abdullah Mansoor was right. You *are* the man I am looking for. My name is Hafiz Mohammed, and you must be Abduweli. *Assalam Alaikum wa Rahmatullah wa Barakatuh*" greeted the middle-aged bearded man.

"*Alaikum Assalam wa Rahmatullah,*" responded Abduweli. Taking the name of Abdullah Mansoor was enough for Abduweli to shed the mantle of caution, and within minutes they got about the business of getting acquainted and updating each other on common topics of interest.

"I want to get to Pakistan to find my father, and to undergo training in the camps there. Will you help me?" enquired Abduweli of this new found acquaintance who seemed to appear as a man of influence where it mattered.

"Reach Turkey first, and we shall see. Some matters will be attended to there that will make your further movement easy." replied Hafiz.

"There are three others with me. All four of us want to get to Pakistan for training." continued Abduweli.

"Sure! All four of you can get to Pakistan through Turkey. Are they friends of yours?" asked Hafiz.

Abduweli shrugged his shoulders and continued, "They are also from back home, but from different parts of the province.

I got to know them while on the way to this place, and now we are friends."

"What will the training in Pakistan be like? Do you know or have you heard?" asked a curious Abduweli.

"Sure! I know. I went through it myself. It is tough, intense, and unforgiving. You get trained in three stages in different camps, in different places. First you are taken into a recruiting camp where they watch you go through some preliminary paces and select suitable candidates for the next phase of training. They separate the wheat from the chaff, if you know what I mean. Those rejected are sent back from where they came. This training lasts for thirty to thirty five days. The instructors are dedicated and committed men – committed to our common cause." Hafiz paused and looked at Abduweli for reactions. He saw only searching eyes and curiosity, combined with a sense of eagerness, written largely all over his face.

"There are many camps for this phase of training and they are all located in Azaad Kashmir between Lahore and Muzaffarabad." continued Hafiz. All this went clear over Abduweli's head as he had no idea where the places mentioned were located. He even had difficulty in trying to remember the names. But he was excited, impressed, and listened attentively.

"From there, on completion of the first phase, the highly motivated and physically fit successful recruits are sent for their main training to three or four camps covering different terrains and conditions, for the next phase. In these camps, carefully selected and fully competent instructors familiarize the recruits with the use of different types of light weapons and explosives, teach them about navigation and map reading, about wireless communications and radio telephony, and other expertise vital for survival during conduct of carefully selected special operations" explained Hafiz.

"Here also, there are a number of drop-outs" he said, "But I do not think you should have problems as you have a good physique, and seem to be intelligent and well motivated. How much of education have you had?" asked Hafiz.

"All that I know is from what I was taught in the *madrasah* in *Korla City* in Bayingolin, while I was staying with my aunt. I can speak, read, and write Pashtu and Mandarin well." he said with some pride. Hafiz nodded his head as he put that bit of information away in his brain.

"Please continue" Abduweli pleaded and Hafiz complied.

"Those who manage to complete the second phase of training go on to the launching camps for the third and final phase of training to become *jihadis* or *fidayeens* to operate in groups of twenty five to thirty, for deployment across the Indo-Pakistan border, in Afghanistan, Iraq or Syria, or in other parts of the world."

"By the way, do not divulge all what I am telling you to anyone here or to those travelling with you. I have told you all this to prepare you for what lies ahead and for you to mentally prepare yourself to train well." advised Hafiz. "You will be my special recruit, and I will have important things for you to do. At the end of your third phase of training, I will come and meet you at the training site. By then you will be ready to be deployed in any part of the world to fight for the 'rights' of the Islamic State." stated Hafiz with a reassuring half smile on his face.

"I want to settle scores with the Chinese and am not particularly excited about fighting anywhere else. They wiped out my family, my relatives, and constantly humiliate my dwindling community. First I want to go to Wazi…Waziristan or Afghanistan …. Wherever … to locate my father. Then I want to train to hit the Chinese where it hurts them the most. " said Abduweli, emphatically.

"We shall see about that. All in good time" said Hafiz, "*Inshallah*, you just might get the type of opportunity you are looking for. On the other hand, you should be prepared to be deployed elsewhere initially. Deployment is based on urgency and immediate requirements of our Party. But, enough of all this for the moment; it is late. Let us go out and eat something and then get to bed. Your landlord has been kind enough to provide me a bed. We will not talk about this any further till we get back. Do not disclose these matters to the other three with you either," he repeated. "They will get to know what they have to, at the appropriate time." He put an arm around Abduweli and led him out of the door and out on the streets.

He did not disclose to this young man that he had worked with his father, who had made the supreme sacrifice, and was now resting with Allah. This was not the right time for that.

They had many more opportunities over the next two days to discuss matters before they parted. Abduweli went on to Turkey and on to Pakistan, while Hafiz Mohammed continued on his recruitment drive to Sulawesi in Indonesia where a pro-ISIS organization existed under the name of *Mujahidin Indonesia Timor.*

Diplomatic Reception

Diplomatic parties in New Delhi were a regular affair and the Head of R&AW got frequently invited to them, not so much for him to pick up bits and pieces of information but for the host and his allies to pick as much as they can from him. One could treat them as social engagements with an opportunity to make new contacts, or just occasions for having a good time in good company. Jimmy had a problem with these parties. He did not like to attend them. He could not decline most of them. He did not drink! The army he had served in tried, his friends tried, his adversaries in his job also tried. None of them succeeded. It ran in his family. All the men-folk in his family were tee-totallers. The sad part was that no one who was told this believed him. They thought he probably wanted to be alert under all situations to illustriously pick up information. After all, wasn't he in the business of gathering intelligence? Jimmy let them draw their own conclusions and did not try to justify this habit of his too much. He was content to hold a glass of sparkling water with a dash of fresh lime, bitters, or lime cordial in it for just that bit of taste and coloring to get by too many questions being put to him. Worse! – He held on to that one glass for the whole evening, topping it up with ice every now and then, to maintain a minimum level. He never took his wife to these parties. He kept her protected from the diplomatic and cloak and dagger world as much as he could.

The evening in the resplendent Roosevelt House – the official residence of the Ambassador in the Embassy on Shanti Path, Chanakyapuri - began pleasantly enough. The US Secretary of State had just concluded her business in India, and was on her way to the Peoples Republic of China the following day on a three-day visit. Naturally, among the elite of the diplomatic corps, the Chinese Ambassador was also present - with his usual dead-pan face. All Chinese did not have dead-pan faces. Only this ambassador specialized in one, opined Jimmy. He moved around, exchanging pleasantries. He was introduced to the Secretary of State who did not show any special interest in him and moved on to the next group with the US Ambassador on her heels. Jimmy made a special effort to walk up to the Chinese Ambassador for a chat after the US Secretary of State had exchanged pleasantries with him and chatted with him for awhile. During the short exchange, Jimmy politely enquired:

"I hope the Indian Naval ships will have no trouble on their return leg from exercising with the Japanese Maritime Defense Forces like they did on their way to Japan."

The Ambassador retorted, "We are very particular about keeping an eye on who is in our waters, and what their business is, just like you are particular about who is in your waters, and what their business is. Surely you cannot call that 'trouble'?"

"No, of course not, Your Excellency." replied Jimmy. "I was thinking of that incident between a US Reconnaissance plane and two Chinese jet fighters in the South China Sea on April 1st, 2001 that resulted in damage to the US plane and loss of a plane and life of a Chinese pilot, when I was referring to 'trouble'."

"That was in 2001. That was long ago. Times have changed," he said as he bowed stiffly and walked away from Jimmy.

Jimmy retreated to the outskirts of the socializing group and watched with detached interest.

"Good evening Mr. Ahuja" said a voice from behind him. Turning around, he found himself staring at the smiling face of his 'tail' on his return flight from Washington, and the man he crossed in the India International Centre, just a few weeks ago.

"Do we know each other?" enquired Jimmy, stretching out his hand to shake the man's hand.

"Yes! We do now. Allow me to introduce myself; my name is Al Turner. I have recently reported to the Embassy here, on a tour of duty. We travelled on the same flights from Washington to New Delhi – remember?"

Jimmy preferred not to, and pretended to look confused. "I can't recollect seeing you on the plane. Anyway, glad to meet you. What duties are you going to perform in the Embassy?"

"I have been assigned to the 'Visa' section. It had to be augmented as the H1B visa rules have changed and there are hordes of Indians outside the Embassy every day; more than the Embassy can handle with its present staff on a day to day basis," he laughed.

My foot! Thought Jimmy, but decided to go along with the game. "Just, one man? Or have they sent a team with you to handle the rush?"

"Well, more are expected in the near future", he stuttered.

"How did you know my name?" asked Jimmy.

"We get a briefing when we report to the Embassy and all the important personage are made known to us" was his laconic reply.

So, he was not ready to open up as yet, concluded Jimmy, and did not press him further. They talked about the weather in Delhi and other inconsequential things, while sizing each other up. A while later, Al Turner, under pretense of wanting to meet someone else from another group of Embassy people, excused himself and moved away from Jimmy. Al Turner, right? I bet that is not his real name mulled Jimmy. Later, from the passenger manifest of the flight that he had asked for, he did find Al Turner on the list. So, he was going to live with that name while in India.

It was speech time. They all made the usual, appropriate noises over the mike – the US Ambassador, the Secretary of State, and the External Affairs Minister of India. Toasts were drunk. Jimmy held up his glass of tinted soda and took sips along with the others. The two National Anthems were played while everyone stood still, and the party ended. Across the room, he saw Gamaliel, the Mossad man, lingering in the crowd. He had pretended not to know or recognize Jimmy altogether, when their eyes met for a brief moment earlier in the evening. He could afford to. Jimmy was new in his chair. Oh! Well! Each to his own, thought Jimmy as he left the US Embassy. Even while he was leaving, from the corner of his eye he saw Gamaliel heading towards Al Turner.

Kaloyanov

Kaloyanov gazed out of his office window, across the valley, at the massive construction work that was in progress on the opposite hill slope of *The Blue Rocks*, with great satisfaction. Despite the strong winds that plague the region, he would be completing the construction in another six months time. Then the money would start coming in and he would be a rich man. First he would have to pay back the money ploughed into the project by his Saudi and Kuwaiti financiers and friends who had generously invested 95 million Euros. After paying the sub-contractors, and clearing dues, he would be left with an impressive sum. In return, he would be providing homes to retirees who would live here in Sliven, in Bulgaria, in a condo that would rival Beverly Hills in the USA. The condo will have a beautiful view of the valley and the town of Sliven below, with its three rivers - *Asenokvska, Novoselska, and Manastirska* – flowing from the hills around, and converging near the town below.

He had done well after retiring from the Intelligence Branch of the Bulgarian army in the rank of a Colonel. Moving quickly to Saudi Arabia, he found a job in a construction company where he steadily learnt the ropes. Being an amiable man, and one quick to make friends, he moved freely with the Saudis, and made many friends. He even had friends in other construction companies like, for example, in the Bin Laden Construction Company, owned by Osama Bin Laden's family in Saudi Arabia. Once having learnt the ropes and confident of moving out on his own in this new-found profession, Kaloyanov came back to Bulgaria to construct this condo overlooking the picturesque town of Sliven.

A short, portly, balding man of 60 years with an imaginary waist-line, he had lived his early years and his military life under the Communist regime in the Intelligence Branch when Bulgaria was under tight control of the Soviet Union. With the break-up of the latter, he quickly settled in the new world where, as he understood it, money was all that mattered. Both systems had their advantages, he reasoned. The first was required to get off the starting blocks on even footing; the second was required to break away from the limitations the first system had. Looking at both, while he preferred the first system earlier, he now was all for the second system. He was after money, and did not mind if it came to him through straight or shady deals as long as it did not bring him trouble.

His marriage turned out to be a disaster, and one he sadly walked out from. The initial years were happy ones, but they did not have any children because he found out after marriage that his wife could not have any. Five years into it, on his return from a tour of duty in Czechoslovakia, he found a stranger with her in his own bed – a Soviet army officer. He threw her out and decided that he was done with the institution of marriage. Oh! He did have relationships with more than one woman off and on after that, but no lasting ones. At sixty, he was still proud of his sexual prowess. Despite his adiposity, women were attracted to him, and his signs of prosperity.

Kaloyanov knew Sliven well. It was a quiet town well known for its health spas. Located about 300 km east of Bulgaria's capital Sofia, around 130 km from the border with Greece, and about the same distance from the border with Turkey, it is not far from the famed Sunny Beach that is well sought out by tourists for a lively holiday in this part of the world. The night life, in particular, drew hordes of young men and women to Sunny Beach from Europe in search of some fun with gay abandon. While in the army, he had served in Sliven and frequently visited Sunny Beach for entertainment.

An old Soviet military base with an arms dump was located in the outskirts of Sliven. There, he had stumbled across abandoned nuclear warheads and plutonium detonators.

He did not disclose his 'find' to anyone. Cold and calculating, and without wasting any time, he moved ten of them secretly out from the abandoned Soviet military dump to Varna, where his mother lived, and stashed them away in a place where they were unlikely to be found. He felt these pieces would fetch him a lot of money at the appropriate time. But he would have to be careful. This, he did as a consequence of an earlier experience he had been through some years back.

While working in Saudi Arabia, he was approached by some friendly Pakistanis. "We would like you to come and attend a meeting where Osama Bin Laden will be speaking" they had said. Since he was at a loose end, he had accepted their invitation and attended the meeting. At the end of that meeting, the Pakistanis introduced him to Osama Bin Laden, and they shook hands. Osama Bin Laden had looked at him perfunctorily, and given a stiff smile. Perhaps this was because he was working in a rival construction company. Perhaps he, Bin Laden, had no interest in him. The meeting was short and nothing came of it, but the next day Laden's assistants had approached him in his residence, late in the evening. Kaloyanov remembered every word of their conversation as if the meeting had taken place only yesterday. "We have come to you on a matter of strict confidence. This is not to be discussed with anyone. Understand? – Anyone!" They had paused for a moment before continuing, "Our leader, whom you met yesterday, would like you to set up a Waste Management Company to process nuclear waste near Kozloduy, a small city on the river Danube, about 120 Km from Sofia, in far eastern Bulgaria – your country. Are you willing to do this? We will fund you and support this venture," they exclaimed. There were two of them. At that time Kozloduy had the country's biggest nuclear power station located on its outskirts. "And why should I be interested in doing this?" asked Kaloyanov. "To help us, and make you rich in the process," they had responded. "We want you to supply some of that nuclear waste to us," they had continued. Kaloyanov caught on very quickly, being a man with an intelligence background. These fellows had obviously wanted the stuff to make 'dirty bombs'! Huge sums of money were discussed and offered. "Give me 48 hours to think this over" was what Kaloyanov had told them. Later he had backed out after making excuses, as he had got cold feet and did not want to get involved with terrorists. But the seed had been planted in his mind that there were takers for nuclear waste who were willing to pay large sums to get their hands on some of it. They would, definitely, pay more for nuclear warheads and plutonium detonators, he concluded.

He gathered his wandering thoughts, stepped out of his construction office, and got into his 1969 model *Bulgaralpine* sports car to drive across to the building site to check out a few things. The Bulgarian car was very special and dear to him as only some one hundred and twenty were ever built. It was a bright red colored convertible with a powerful engine under the bonnet. Everyone in the locality knew he owned it, and it always announced his arrival even before he stepped out of it. It was a beautiful Friday evening, and with the week-end looming ahead, he decided to drive down to Sunny Beach after his work for the day, to indulge in some debauchery. Living all by himself, he had very little else by way of entertainment to keep him amused. He had only one, possibly two, friends in Sliven, and both were married and thoroughly domesticated. His girlfriends were in Sunny Beach, and he believed in safety in numbers. Yet he visited them selectively. His male friends – his close buddies – were in Varna. Looking back over the years, he was happy with his steady progress in acquiring wealth, and his present style of living. The past did occasionally visit him. That was inevitable as he had made many contacts while he was an intelligence officer in the army. Those 'acquaintances' would contact him now and then, asking for favors in the line of work they had retained. Being helpful by nature, Kaloyanov obliged them to the extent possible. As a result, they wouldn't stop coming to him, despite being fully aware of the fact that his influence as a former intelligence officer was steadily waning with the passage of time.

Turbulent Waters – Posturing Navies

The Indian Task Group, returning from Japan, had just sailed through the Taiwan Strait and was about to cross the Tropic of Cancer and enter the South China Sea.

The INS Mysore was the first to pick up a submarine contact ahead, which was soon thereafter also picked up by the INS Delhi. Both began tracking the submarine and her movements. These were submarine infested waters they were transiting. Rear Admiral Zora Singh, the Indian Task Group Commander, peered through the screen of INS Delhi's bridge out into the wide open ocean ahead. To the others on the bridge, it appeared as if he had spotted something that they hadn't, and ten pairs of eyes, with binoculars affixed, peered in the same direction, vying with each other to be the first to report whatever was supposedly attracting the Admiral's attention.

Suddenly the Officer of the Watch announced, "Submarine periscope fine on the starboard bow! Range about six miles." This was not a visual sighting but one picked up on the radar screen.

The Officer of the Watch again announced, "Periscope disappeared. Submarine appears to have gone deep."

It could have been a submarine belonging to the Taiwanese navy or the navy of mainland China. The three ships were in an arrow head formation and had their sonar sets switched on in a passive, listening, mode, which was the mode they adopt when transiting through international waters in peace-time. They also had only their navigational radars switched on under these conditions. The formation of three ships altered course to port, away from the submarine. Additional sensors were now switched on to continue tracking the submarine passively.

Masking procedures were introduced to deny the submarine sensitive information about the ships. This was routine procedure.

The Admiral's action had been mechanical; he hadn't sighted anything. In fact his thoughts were elsewhere. Mentally he was reviewing the positives of his visit with this Task Group to Japan, the many official 'calls' he had made, his interactions with those in Japan who mattered, the bridges of friendship established as a result of the visit, the exercises at sea they had with the Japanese Maritime Self Defense Force units, discussions on Chinese expansionist policies, so on and so forth. From his point of view, it had been a very successful visit and there was much that he had to report about, once he got back to India. He abruptly got up from his chair and went to have a look at the Chart on the Navigator's Chart Table. He hoped this time there would be no trouble from the Chinese. They had one more visit – to Haiphong in Vietnam – before they headed home.

A three-day bi-lateral exercise was also scheduled in the Gulf of Tonkin with some ships and a submarine of the Vietnamese navy. The waters were shallow in the Gulf of Tonkin, with varying densities due to the meeting of sea water and the outflow of fresh water from the rivers into the gulf. This would make submarine operations tricky and challenging and it would be interesting to see how the Vietnamese submarine was going to cope with these conditions, and perform.

"Admiral Sir! Black Panther is in touch and will be joining us in twenty five minutes", reported the Captain of INS Delhi to the Admiral.

"Very Good!" he responded in true nautical style. "Ask him to investigate this submarine contact and then rejoin us. When is the Neptune joining us?" he enquired.

"She is expected to join us in two hours' time. She is already airborne from the Nicobar Islands and heading our way, Sir", continued the Captain.

"Very Good," was the Admiral's reply again. "I shall go to my cabin now. Let me know when she joins us" said the Admiral as he left the bridge.

The returning Indian Task Group from Japan was once again met by an Indian P8i-Neptune maritime reconnaissance aircraft, as scheduled, as the formation came abreast of Hong Kong. Like an albatross, the maritime aircraft led the way through the South China Sea into the Gulf of Tonkin, with all her passive detection sensors switched on. They were shadowed at a discreet distance by a Chinese Type 052C destroyer. She remained closer to the Chinese coastline and ran a parallel course to that of the Indian Task Group. There was no 'challenge' or untoward incident. The Black Panther rejoined the formation and reported that the submarine they had picked up earlier belonged to the Taiwanese navy.

A single US Navy guided missile destroyer was sighted as the Task Group neared the Paracel Group of islands that were claimed by China, Taiwan, and Vietnam, but in full possession of China. The normal courtesies between warships of different navies were exchanged. She too had a Chinese Type 052C destroyer following her at a discreet distance. The US Navy send their ships into the South China Sea on a regular basis just to make a statement that the sea did not 'belong' to any one particular country.

The Task Group wended its way past Chinese fishing boats by the hundreds. The Chinese were the biggest consumers of marine produce in the world. Their fishing boats flooded the South China Sea and the Gulf of Tonkin, and did not stop there. Chinese fishing vessels have been regularly sighted fishing in far-off Argentinean waters, and other such remote seas. As the Task Group neared the Gulf of Tonkin, they came across an equal number of Vietnamese fishing craft. There was a prominent and distinct difference in construction and appearance between the fishing vessels of the two countries. The Chinese fishing vessels were much larger. There was an ongoing fishing war between the two countries. Not liking the presence of Vietnamese fishing boats in the areas they consider their private zone, the larger Chinese fishing boats often rammed and sank the smaller Vietnamese boats.

Once the Task Group entered Vietnamese shallow waters of 70 meters depth and less, the Black Panther turned around and returned to her patrolling duties in deeper waters of the South China Sea, following and tracking the withdrawing unsuspecting Chinese destroyer en route. The Neptune aircraft was also detached and sent back to the Nicobar Islands. Relations were not smooth between China and Vietnam, and the visit by Indian ships off and on to show solidarity with their old and trusted friend in this region was disliked by mainland China.

The Vietnam navy had seized a Chinese fishing vessel that had encroached into its territorial waters, and towed it into the port of Haiphong some months ago. According to Vietnam media, the Chinese boat was disguised as a fishing boat but was transporting diesel oil that was to be sold to Chinese fishing boats operating illegally in Vietnamese waters. It was stopped near the Vietnamese island of Bach Long Vi and the Chinese island of Hainan. Vietnam rarely seized Chinese boats. They normally chased them away. This was an exception. Rear Admiral Zora Singh, the Indian Task Group Commander, was briefed about the fishing 'war' by the Commander of Haiphong, when he called on him in his office. The Admiral also visited the Indian satellite tracking station that was functioning from Vietnam.

Even while the bi-lateral exercises between the two friendly navies took off, a near explosive situation developed near the Spratly Islands that prematurely terminated the Indo-Vietnamese exercises. A Chinese Coast Guard vessel rammed and sank five Vietnamese fishing vessels in one day. Some surviving Vietnamese fishing vessels in the vicinity of Spratly Islands managed to get away with video recordings of some of those rammings. These were relayed quickly to mainland Vietnam. The incident stirred anti- China protests and riots in Hanoi, Haiphong, and Ho Chi Minh cities. The Chinese embassy in Hanoi was stormed by rioters leading to four deaths that included one of a Vietnamese office staff employed there. The Chinese Coast Guard vessel turned around and headed for her base in Yulin to attend to the damages caused by the rammings, but did not quite get there. She mysteriously exploded in mid-ocean and sank. Chinese authorities believed that this was an action carried out in retaliation by a submarine belonging to the Vietnamese Navy. There was no evidence to suggest this, but it led the Chinese navy to launch anti submarine forces in the area to locate and destroy the 'attacker'. Their aircraft carrier, the *Liaoning*, on her way to Yulin from Qingdao, had just cleared the Taiwan Strait. She, with her escorts was diverted to join the Chinese anti submarine forces off the Spratly Islands. She arrived the following morning and her aircraft were launched to posture against the Vietnamese navy that, having terminated their exercises with the Indian Navy, had headed south towards the Spratly Islands. Unknown to this Chinese Task Force, they were tailed by the Black Panther for a good part of the distance, revealing all their vital signatures without even being aware of their giveaways. Two days after the sinking of the Chinese Coast Guard vessel, and a day after the *Liaoning* entered the arena, the US Navy sent her aircraft carrier, *USS George Washington,* and her escorts to the same area to join their lone destroyer already present in the area. The Indian Navy's Task Group was directed by New Delhi to join the US forces and work with them.

While the South China Sea was teeming with warships and aircraft in aggressive postures, matters were taken up at diplomatic levels between Vietnam and China in an attempt to defuse the situation. This only led to angry verbal exchanges. Again through diplomatic channels, but this time by the Americans, the Chinese were approached and advised to hold back. They, the US government, were told to stop meddling in matters that were of no concern of theirs. Countries began taking sides beginning with ASEAN, Australia, Japan, and South Korea. One by one, Ambassadors were summoned by host governments and handed protest letters. Some countries threatened to impose economic embargos on China. Anti-China protests were voiced in many countries across the world. To restore normalcy, the only way was by providing China with a face saving move. This had to be done quickly, as the South China Sea was like a tinder box about to explode.

At this stage, the UN Security Council (UNSC) stepped in and called for an emergency meeting preceded by a directive that all naval forces in the South China Sea withdraw to their original positions before this incident had triggered off actions. The Vietnamese navy turned and headed for the Gulf of Tonkin; the Chinese navy entered Yulin harbor; the US Navy entered Tsoying Naval Base in Taiwan. There was no mention of anyone's submarines and where they were or were not deployed. The matter was discussed by the UNSC, and on this occasion the situation was diffused temporarily, with no permanent solution arrived at.

The Indian Task Group under the command of Rear Admiral Zora Singh departed from the South China Sea, heading home. A few weeks after their departure, another Indian Flotilla, on its return from Russian and Korean ports, was to visit Vietnam, Malaysia, and Singapore.

The Opening Gambit

After he received the 'go-ahead' from the Prime Minister, Jimmy contacted Gamaliel and brought forward their meeting – a meeting that was originally scheduled in the Taj Palace Hotel on Sardar Patel Marg, in a private room, for later in the month. They met in the same venue but earlier, after taking all the normal precautions. Room Service was asked to send up some soft and hard drinks with some munchies. An exchange of pleasantries followed by the usual small talk took place, and then Jimmy got to the point.

"Are you aware of the incident that took place recently in the South China Sea between an Indian Naval Task Force on its way to Japan, and the PLA (Navy)? That was before the other incident of the Chinese Coast Guard ship sinking after an explosion."

Gamaliel nodded and added, "That area is a hot bed and will remain so for some years to come. Besides, you and the Americans are also getting sucked into it."

"We have our friends there who cannot be let down, and we support their stand. Also, by helping them, and working with them, we will be helping ourselves" responded Jimmy.

"You are not doing enough" muttered Gamaliel under his breath.

"What do you feel is the way ahead towards arriving at a solution?" he prodded Gamaliel.

"The solutions can be many; that is, if a solution is immediately required by all" responded Gamaliel thoughtfully as he took a deep sip of Glenfiddich from his glass. "ASEAN concedes to the Chinese stand and backs out; the Chinese accedes to request for international shipping exercising 'Right of

Innocent Passage' through the South China Sea in return; India and the US back off; joint development by neighboring states. But, these things will not happen as they are unacceptable to the interested parties who are opposed to China's hegemonistic plans for the region. Neither would it be acceptable to China. For that matter, they will not be acceptable to the US and India either" he said raising his glass and pointing it towards Jimmy.

"So?" – Jimmy wanted him to continue.

"So, the answer is to get the Chinese to slow down their plans by misadventure, without getting into a serious fracas with them that could lead to dangerous consequences for all in the region" said Gamaliel with a wink. Jimmy was getting him onto the line of thinking he was looking for.

"There are huge reserves of gas and oil in the region; the atolls and islands of Spratly and Paracel are being beefed up with reclamations and military presence; and the island of Hainan is being developed into a huge naval base that will be used as a stepping stone into the Indian Ocean" went on Jimmy as he stared into his half glass of soda with a dash of lime. "No country save the United States of America can challenge these developments."

"Why don't you send your R&AW team there to sabotage some of their works?" asked Gamaliel mischievously.

"No way - our government will not even think of it. The idea is simply preposterous! In any case, we don't work that way. We don't have a team to do such things" said Jimmy, but was inwardly happy that the discussions were going the way it was.

"Neither do we have a team in Mossad for such jobs. But we get it done by supporters or sympathizers, or even by our armed forces if this is in our national interest." retorted Gamaliel. "Remember Entebbe?"

Now Jimmy had him where he wanted him. "Listen! I have an idea. But I want your help." Jimmy then went on to explain the kind of help he had in mind, and Gamaliel listened with great interest. When Jimmy had finished, Gamaliel stared at Jimmy for a long while and then slowly refilled his glass from the Glenfiddich bottle. He broke the silence and asked,

"You have obviously been mulling this over in your mind for quite awhile, haven't you? How do you know about the consignment, and where it is? You are not giving me your whole plan or line of thinking; you want me to help you with only a part of it. And what's in it for my country, and for my organization? Why should we put our necks on the block?"

"We are two nations that stand by each other in troubled times. Remember? We have always supported you in international forums, the Palestinian situation notwithstanding. It will not be for the first time that you would be doing us a favor. Remember your help during the Kargil war when we fought to evacuate Pakistan soldiers entrenched there? What was in it for you? Your government got some money and, more importantly, a lot of gratitude and goodwill from our country for all the help given. In any case, you could deny any involvement in this operation should you be drawn into a situation where you may have to make a statement" replied Jimmy.

Gamaliel was right. Jimmy was being careful not to reveal the whole plan to him, but only the part where his organization's help would be needed.

"Are you serious? You are not drinking and so I cannot even say this is a 'spirited' inspiration," stated Gamaliel. Jimmy nodded emphatically.

"Give me time. I need to think this over and discuss it with my authorities back home. They will probably not want to get into this. There is nothing in it for us but trouble and risks, as I see it. It is not going to be very easy. It has many deep complications. I shall get back to you. In the meantime, let this remain only between you and me. Do not discuss this with your team. Do not even mention to your bosses that you have approached me. By the way, did you get any directive from your higher ups to approach me? Is that why you advanced our meeting?" he enquired.

What team? There is no team yet. I am alone in this so far, thought Jimmy to himself. His thoughts were interrupted by Gamaliel, who was continuing with his monologue,

"This is madness. Have you, meaning your government, discussed this with the Americans?" he asked, to which Jimmy shook his head in the negative.

"Shouldn't you be consulting them?" he pursued.

"If the Americans want to do anything, they will do it by themselves, now or at a moment of their choosing, without anybody's help" replied Jimmy. "No! I don't want them involved" he lied.

"Look Gamaliel, my friend; this idea has only just struck me after you just made that statement. Your idea is a good one. I want to explore the possibilities of developing it into a workable solution. But that will depend on how far you are willing to go. I knew about the consignment for quite some time, and I know you know about it too. We are in the same profession. Remember? Information about it was leaked some time back. Obviously, I have not spoken about this to anyone in my government. Why am I ready to stick my head out and risking putting it on the blocks? Maybe it is because of who I am and the career I have had. Maybe, sitting with you here, I am being inspired. I want to think this over more deeply and work on it, and in that process, I am asking you if you will do what I have just requested you to do. Give me a positive answer and I will proceed with my plans. Give me a negative answer and I shall drop it. Got it?"

Glenfiddich needed re-charging, and Gamaliel proceeded to do this with fuss and much ado. Jimmy is lying, he thought to himself; he would not have advanced this meeting or broached this subject without a 'go-ahead' from his authorities. What are the Indians up to? This is certainly not like them. Who has put them onto this? He wondered.

"Whatever you are doing – I wish you luck. But one thing I will confess. I like it!" said Gamaliel with a wink and a twinkle in his eyes that had nothing to do with the effects of the malt, from the Valley of the Deer, that he had been imbibing. He downed his glass fast and Jimmy joined him by emptying his.

On that note they decided to part. The room was booked for more than a day and so they did not have to check-out. They locked it and left, each going their separate ways, so as not to be seen together.

The Training Camps

Abduweli's four month long journey from Bayingolin finally came to a halt in early February when he, along with the other two Uighur, Yusup and Ehmet, arrived in Muridke, near Lahore in Pakistan. It was an arduous journey that could only be completed with determination and steadfastness of purpose. Muridke is a major commercial city located along the Grand Trunk Road that runs north-south through the bigger cities of Pakistan. Much of Muridke's social and cultural life leans heavily on neighboring Lahore. It is also the Headquarters of the *Lashkar–e-Taiba* (LET) and *Markaz Ad-Dawa-wal-Irshad* operating from within Pakistan. Both organizations had been banned internationally, but continued to enjoy protection in that country. The fourth man in Aduweli's group, Erkin, dropped out and stayed back in Thailand to seek his fortune there after getting drawn to the ways of the flesh found all too easily in Bangkok's local massage parlors, clubs, its underworld, and the likes.

In Turkey, Abduweli found that there was a new problem for Uighur who wanted to enroll in training camps in Pakistan. They were debarred from coming into the country. The Chinese had been pressurizing Pakistan to stop accepting Uighur volunteers for training in their terrorist camps as they were harming Chinese interests in the province of Xinjiang. In return, they were giving Pakistan strong support against accusations of harboring and training terrorists in international forums. Pakistan was also suspicious of outsiders enrolling, after repeated drone attacks by the US practically annihilated many trainees in camps. They believed that spies were being sent to give inside information that helped in directing accurate drone strikes. The flip side of the coin was that they also wanted to train more and more men to use them against India, in Afghanistan, and to operate with the ISIS in other parts of the world. To appease their Chinese 'all-weather' friends, Uighur separatists were therefore restricted from entering Pakistan and needed a 'godfather' who would recommend and promote entry for a selected few. For Abduweli, that godfather was Abdullah Mansoor from the *Turkistan Islamic Party* who had some influence with the authorities in Muridke. Sitting in Turkey, Abduweli had to contact Abdullah Mansoor to put in a word for him and the other two with him, for granting entry. All the necessary influence, lies, and bluffs had to be used to make this possible. Anyway, here he was with his two friends in Pakistan, ready to commence his training, and more importantly, to locate and meet his father.

There were around forty training camps at any one time spread all over Pakistan and in Azad Kashmir. The camps comprised of small groups dispersed over a large area, in temporary shelters, hidden from satellite detection, and known to few. Classes were conducted in abandoned schools or houses offered by people around. Around twenty persons formed a class.

The training was meticulous. Abduweli found the Muridke training camp professionally competent, unforgiving, and tough. The trainees were constantly shifted around so that no permanence in location could be discerned. One day they were in Mohalla Faiz Madina, another day in Afzal Colony, a third day in Mohalla Gaddafi Park, a few days later in Mohalla Chaitian, and so on. Pashtu was the language for instructions and he had to better his knowledge of the language quickly. They were paid well and fed well during training. The '*Daura-e-Suffa*', as the camp was referred to, involved daily morning prayers and recitations from the Koran commencing at 4:00am, followed by indoctrination and lectures on the essence, necessity, and benefits of *Jihad*. Religious discourses followed. Very senior members of LET conducted these sessions, in Muridke. Sometimes, the Pakistani Army's ISI sent their personnel to conduct classes. During the day they would be put through vehicle driving classes on two, three, and four wheelers, toning up exercises, and physical drills to build up stamina in preparation for acquiring skills they were going to be trained for in the next phase. After lunch they would again assemble for prayers. Indoctrination sessions were again conducted in the evenings accompanied by prayers. Suitably doctored or even un-doctored videos were shown to build up hatred against the outside world and drive home the importance of getting to become a *fidayeen* or a *jihadi,* and the difference between the two. This '*Daura-e-Suffa*' camp lasted for three weeks.

On completion of this phase of training, Abduweli, Ehmet and Yusup found themselves along with ten other successful candidates, transported north, to Muzaffarabad. This city is located in the hills of Mansehra in the what is referred to by Pakistan as the capital of Azad Jammu and Kashmir, and by neighboring India as a town in Pakistan Occupied Kashmir. The city is built around the confluence of the Neelum and Jhelum rivers in picturesque, hilly surroundings. The training, referred to as the '*Daura-e-Aam*' (General Session), was scheduled in and around this city and its hills in '*Umm-al-Qura*' training camps. The Neelum valley was a favorite spot to train in. Just across the Line of Control were the Indian villages of Tithwal and Kupwara. Camp locations were referred to by names such as Manastaya/ Match Factory, Chelabandi, Abdul-Bin- Masud and Balakot. There were many more. The three Uighur bonded well during training, thanks to the fact that they were the only Uighur in the whole group. They frequently egged and helped each other during the course too. Again, a source of great disappointment to Abduweli was that no one was able to tell him about the whereabouts of his father. Refusing to believe that he could probably have gone to be with his Maker, Abduweli clung on to the belief that he must have changed his name and was now living under a different name or operating elsewhere. Perhaps he was a prisoner somewhere. He kept hoping and making enquiries about the whereabouts of Uighur instructors and trainees, but, disappointingly, drew a blank everywhere. No one knew his father by the name he was calling him by.

They were taught how to handle an AK-47 rifle and other Chinese small arms like the QBZ-95 Bull pup Assault Rifle of 5.8mm caliber, the QSZ-92 Pistol of 5.8mm caliber, QCW-05 Submachine Gun, CS-LR3 Sniper Rifles and grenades. All these arms and ammunition were supplied indirectly by the Pakistan army to these training camps. The physical training also got tough and included training to fight and survive against lethal opposition, in tough and varied terrains. During this phase, one of the trainees disobeyed orders and stood up just to state that he had had enough. He was riddled by a hail of bullets that he was supposed to have crawled under. It shocked the rest of them to meticulously follow what was taught to them. Abduweli successfully completed this very rigorous and physically demanding course and so did the other two Uighur, Yusup and Ehmet. Having done both three-week courses successfully, the three Uighur were sent to attend the '*Daura-e-Khaas*' (Special Course), along with a dwindled number of other successful candidates.

The three months advanced combat '*Daura-e-Khaas*' course was the most rigorous and toughest of them all. It was conducted in the mountainous regions higher up and beyond the hills of Mansehra on the Balakot side of Muzaffarabad, and in other parts of Azad Kashmir. It included more physical training, classes on guerilla warfare and street fighting; familiarization with, and use of, various types of more advanced weapons; instructions on the use of mortars, rocket launchers, and grenades; commando training; maritime training; sabotage, counter-intelligence, making various explosive devices (IEDs); how to interrogate captives, and a detailed course on the use of communication equipment. A three-day survival exercise where they had to hide, with their Instructors chasing and hunting them down, culminated the training. The trainees who outdid their instructors were rewarded. It was not necessary for everyone to be taught all the skills. Those earmarked for operations on land, for example, did not have to go through the maritime training. The candidates were now divided into *jihadi* squads, *seaward attack* squads, *fidayeen* squads, and the likes, and given intense training in their selected fields. Religious indoctrination continued. The Uighur trio was put for training with the *fidayeen* squads.

During this last part of training, Abduweli suddenly found himself face-to-face with Hafiz Mohammed one day. He couldn't believe his eyes! He remembered Hafiz telling him, in Bangkok, that he would come and meet him during the third phase of his training, but had not taken it seriously at that time. Now here he was, staring at him and looking very much the same.

"How is it going so far? Did I not tell you that you would make it to this stage?" exclaimed a delighted Hafiz with a broad grin on his face. He moved closer to hug Abduweli who promptly pushed him and stepped back and away from him. There was no sense of joy or delight on the countenance of the latter.

"Where is my father?" asked Abduweli. "Is he alive? Is he operating under a different name? How come no one in any of the camps is able to tell me of his whereabouts? How come they are not able to confirm whether he is alive or dead?" This volley of questions, directed at Hafiz was accompanied by an angry, cold, look of a man who had been betrayed.

"Easy boy! Easy! Come with me" said the older Hafiz. He drew him away from the rest, out of hearing distance. Then, holding him by the shoulders, he looked directly into his eyes and said,

"I knew your father well. I worked with him. In fact, I would not have been alive today but for him. We were together when we went into Afghanistan. I was injured and left behind to fend for myself when the others withdrew after a raid. It was your father who came back for me and dragged me back to safety, and later took me for medical attention. He was a very brave man, and a very good fighter. Later, I came to know that while he was conducting training classes in South Waziristan, the Americans carried out a drone strike and your father was killed. He is now with Allah, resting, and at peace. Yes, he was known by a different name here."

"You liar! You are not telling me the truth," screamed Abduweli as he fell upon Hafiz and grappled with him. Both rolled on the ground with the attacker trying to throttle the defender. The others, seeing this commotion quickly ran and separated the two.

A struggling Abduweli, held back by three of his colleagues, stared at Hafiz with bloodshot eyes for a long time, wanting to believe that what he had just heard was all a lie.

"Did you know this when we met in Bangkok?" he asked angrily.

"Yes. I did" replied a panting and puffing Hafiz truthfully, as he gathered himself.

"Then why did you not tell me?" asked Abduweli breathing heavily and struggling to break away and get back at Hafiz again.

"Because I knew you would want to avenge his death, for which you would have to undergo this training. I wanted you to finish this training so that you have the competence to avenge his killing, the killing of your mother, the killing of your siblings, and the many Uighur in Xinjiang. For that, the Americans cannot be your target. Your target is the Chinese. Now listen to me very carefully. I will say this only once. After your present training is finished, I am going to get you and your other two countrymen out of here and back to Turkey. The Pakistanis will be relieved. I have a task for the three of you that will help you avenge the extermination of your family by the Chinese. Abdullah Mansoor from the *Turkistan Islamic Party* has approved this. You three will be sent to Istanbul by an indirect and not-so-noticeable route. I will meet the three of you in Istanbul, when you get there, and brief you further."

With that, Hafiz Mohammed dusted his clothes and shuffled away. A stunned Abduweli was left staring into distant space, copious tears of anger and sadness rolling down his cheeks. That his father was no more was a severe blow to him. He found it difficult to accept, although every now and then he had tried to reconcile to the possibility that he was no more. Each time such a feeling crept into his mind he would dismiss it and search anew. He wanted to kill Hafiz Mohammed today and would have done so, had others not intervened! In time he would accept and believe that the only way he could get his revenge on the Chinese was through the Hafiz Mohammed route.

To Varna

During one of those rare, free-from-work weekends that he got, Kaloyanov drove from Sliven to Varna, ostensibly to see his ageing mother. That of course he would do, but he had another purpose this time, and that 'purpose' was in a sturdy box that he had loaded in the car boot the previous night when no one was around. It was heavy for him to carry from the house to his garage comfortably, so he used a hand cart that almost woke up the neighborhood with its squeaking wheels. Damn! He reminded himself that he must oil the wheel bearings when he got back.

There were two routes that he could take to drive to Varna. One was over flat terrain for most of the way, on the A1 highway. It would take him almost up to the sea coast and to Sunny Beach from where he would turn on to the A5 to Shumen and then, through some hilly countryside, proceed to Varna. It was around 220 Km in all and normally took him three hours if he drove non-stop to Varna. He took this route during tourist season so that he could do some 'bird-watching' in Sunny Beach en route, and with a bit of luck, get some 'excitement' thrown in. As a consequence, he invariably took much longer than three hours to reach Varna. Compared to Sunny Beach with its many tourists from all over the world, Sliven was a quiet place. Most of the residents in Sliven were Bulgarians, but apart from them there was a noticeable population of Romanian gypsies, Turks, and a sprinkling of Armenians. Tourists were few and far between and mostly those coming to treat diseases of the nervous system and liver by dipping in the many mineral *baths* in town. For a bit of fun and excitement, Kaloyanov always headed to Sunny Beach on a regular basis. It was the country's liveliest resort with an 8 Km long beach, lined with thousands of restaurants and nightclubs, and with tourist-filled high-rise buildings overlooking the vast sandy waterfront stretch. One could always get a room there for a 'one night stand' and then move on.

The other route to Varna was through the lower reaches of the Balkan ranges on the A2 highway. It had less traffic and was quieter, but was marginally longer. Yet it was quicker. He could get to Varna at least fifteen minutes earlier. Both the routes met up at Shumen for the final lap to Varna together. With the 'luggage' he had, Kaloyanov opted to take the second, hilly, route. He would be driving through very small towns like Sungurlare and Smyadovo tucked away in the hills, looking as dainty as villages in children's picture books. It had its scenic beauty admitted Kaloyanov, with its winding roads and picturesque countryside, but describing it as 'pretty' was a matter of opinion. He found the objects of his desires in Sunny Beach prettier! Sex without love is an empty experience, but as empty experiences go it's a pretty good one, he always reasoned. The twists and turns kept him intent on his driving, and once he crossed over the crest of these ranges and into Shumen, he pulled over for a cup of coffee, keeping a watchful eye on his parked car on the kerb.

How he got the contents now lying in the boot of his car was a story by itself. He did not go looking for it. His dealings with the murky world of underground hoodlums during his days as an Intelligence Officer had helped him retain many connections. It was offered to him by some Chechen separatists from across the Romanian border. They had contacted him indirectly with the offer some months back. They needed money. Kaloyanov saw opportunities for making money out of this purchase, and negotiated well before the items reached him. He now had to store the items away safely and look for prospective customers. He hadn't as yet managed to sell the earlier 'goods' he had taken from Sliven to Varna. However, he was not too worried. Prospective customers kept making tender, oblique, enquiries about the availability of such items. They were not desirable people to do business with, but were willing to pay good money. So far he had been saying that the items were not in his possession, but he could make enquiries. He was waiting for the right price. He was an old 'pro' at this game.

He was almost there now. He had just driven past Varna's airport on his right and was entering the city limits. A little further and he turned left to get off the A2 highway and head for the well-known Techno-market. At the Techno-market he turned right on to Tsar Osvobiditel Street and went down that road till he turned left to Boulevard Republika. His mother's house was not far now.

Nostalgia always set in every time Kaloyanov came to Varna. Memories of his childhood would come rushing back in waves. At that age and stage, the deficiencies of the Communist system did not affect him, though it told on his parents. While they had a hard time making both ends meet, Kaloyanov – their only child – had a happy childhood, good schooling, and many good friends throughout his school years. His father had worked in a factory, building bodies for buses that were used across the length and breadth of Warsaw Pact countries, and even in the Soviet Union. An accident in the factory took his life. Kaloyanov was fourteen years old at that time. His mother, Elisaveta, who worked in the grocery store not far from their residence, saw him through school and into conscription for military service. Thereafter, she continued to live in the same house, but alone, and worked till she was retired and given a monthly pension. Now in her eighties, she was fiercely independent, very active for her age, and upheld the value system of the Communist regime she was brought up in. She did not approve of her son's nefarious activities after he left the army. She did not approve of his greed for money – the root of all evil! She did not forgive him for walking away from his marriage and depriving her of the pleasures of holding grandchildren on her lap.

"Hallo Mama!" he greeted her with a huge bear hug as she opened the door in answer to the call-bell.

"Oh! My son! It is you. I was expecting my neighbor to drop in with some home-made jam she said she would be bringing across", she said with a smile. She kissed him and led him into the sitting room, waiving him on to a chair.

"What brings you away from Sliven this time?" she asked, "And how is the construction work progressing?"

"Progressing well, Mama…..progressing well." He replied. "I have work in the port, here. Some shipment has arrived for me and I have to get it cleared and moved to Sliven by next week" he lied, while critically giving his mother the once over. She appeared to be a wee bit frailer than the last time he saw her, and that was three months ago. But she seemed well enough.

"Go upstairs and wash up and I shall get some lunch ready for you." She smiled. "You are lucky; I have just stocked up yesterday, and have some quick, ready to eat packets. I had made some Hungarian goulash for myself that you can also share. Off with you now", and she moved to the kitchen.

Kalyanov went upstairs to what used to be his bedroom as a kid. There were lots of his things still arranged and kept around to remind him that he belonged here once, but sadly not anymore. He parted the window curtain to glance down to see his car was safe, and then made a phone call on his mobile to a local number.

"I shall be there by six o'clock. Both of you be there." He whispered, in a muffled voice that 'they' recognized. He disconnected the phone and deleted the number. Then he went to the bathroom for a wash.

Lunch was home-cooked and he loved it. His mother kept talking non-stop, and he kept replying in monosyllables as his mind was elsewhere. He must get there under cover of darkness, after making sure he was not being followed. This had to be done quickly, and he should be back in time for supper – a late supper – so that his mother's suspicions, on more than one score, were not aroused.

"Mama, I shall be going down to the harbor now. My work may take awhile, but I shall be back for a late supper. That goulash was nice. Keep some for me tonight" he winked, gave his mother a peck on the cheek, and left.

He drove back onto Tsar Osvobiditel Street and turned left this time. 'Right' was the way back to Shumen. He continued on that road, leaving Vazrazhdane I and II on his left and Mladost II on his right. These were residential layouts. Continuing further, he passed Pchelina, another residential layout, on his left and turned left away from the main Tsar Osvobiditel Street and out of Varna, heading north on a country road. He was now in open country with woods and tilled fields on either side. It had got dark and he had to switch his headlights on. He passed the tiny village of Kamenar on his right and kept on the same road but slowed down, looking all the while for an approach road to a big isolated farmhouse on his right. There it was! He turned into it flashing his headlights in accordance with a pre-arranged signal which was reciprocated by a torch signal with a different code. It was a long driveway. He drove in. Kosta, and Stefan, his classmates from school who enlisted in the army with him, and friends he could trust his life with, were waiting for him. Tight hugs, kisses and back-slapping followed as he was led into their verandah where three wooden benches were awaiting them. Stefan and Kosta jointly owned the farm and stayed and worked in it alternatively. It needed a lot of work. They were growing wheat, barley, and corn and the yields were poor. They were just about breaking even with all their efforts and hard work. Some day they hoped to make money from it. Their families lived in Varna and would come over to the farm as a week-end getaway place to relax in. Both their wives worked in Varna.

After the initial tete-a-tete, Kaloyanov asked them to take him to the barn.

"I do not have much time now as I have an anxious mother awaiting my return, and she just might call the police if she feels I am lost or if her food is getting cold" he winked at them.

All three unloaded his car boot and carried the sturdy box into the barn. The floorboards in one corner were removed, revealing steps leading down into an underground chamber. The three of them went down, with Stefan leading the way with a torch.

"What's in the box?" asked Kosta.

"Some of the same stuff that I brought earlier" replied Kaloyanov with a wink. Stefan whistled in a soft tone.

In the cellar down below was Kaloyanov's earlier 'loot'. The new consignment was added to it. They quickly came up, sealed the floor boards, spread hay over them, and emerged from the barn with the torch switched off.

"When?" asked Kosta.

"Soon! There are enquiries. Be patient" lied Kaloyanov.

They bade farewell and Kaloyanov drove back to his mother's house. What would I do without these friends? He wondered. They were totally reliable and trustworthy. He would be sharing his spoils three-ways with them when he raked in the money. That was agreed upon right from the beginning, and Kaloyanov wouldn't want it any other way.

The Dragon Stirs

March marks the end of winter and the turnaround for spring in Beijing. The weather is therefore changeable and unpredictable – now cold; now windy; now hit by a sandstorm; or now bright and sunny. The temperatures swing between 12 and 6 degrees Celsius, making it difficult to decide what to wear. Trees and flowers show early signs of budding, and with the central heating turned off on 15th March, everyone looked forward to an early spring.

Xin Sheng Zong, The Minister of State Security, was a disturbed man this morning even before he got to his office. The Korean Central Television had announced during its morning broadcast that a terrorist attack in Guangzhou was imminent. How did the North Koreans get this piece of information when he, the Minister of State Security and the Head of China's Intelligence Agency, had not heard about it at all? What was the authenticity of this public proclamation? And why should the North Korean Ambassador personally ring him up and give him this bit of information even while he was dressing up for office? Had he rung others who were higher up in the hierarchy too? He wondered, as he looked out of the window. His chauffer driven car had just passed the Beijing Zoo. The Summer Palace was just ahead. At the Xiyuan (Western Garden) intersection, the driver turned left and they entered his Headquarters. There were no signs posted around to show up his office. The nearest signboard was that of the Institute of Traditional Chinese Medicine which was across his office, on the other side of the road. The elevator from the basement parking area took him up to his floor and he walked unusually fast, almost stumbling on the way, and entered his 'den'.

He reached for his phone even before he had settled down in his chair and dialed the number of the Head of the Domestic

Affairs Bureau. The office had secure lines that were reliable and therefore preferable on such matters to the mobile phone in his pocket. There was no answer! He punched in his Deputy's number. No answer again! He looked at his watch. He had, inadvertently, come half an hour earlier. The others had not come in as yet. No wonder he found the car park almost empty! He would have to wait. Drumming his fingers on the table, he looked around for something to do. He dialed his top man in Guangzhou who, fortunately, was already in his chair. Good man! He learnt from him that there was no information of any terrorist attack in Guangzhou or anywhere in Guangdong district.

Sometime later, when Wang Jing Li, the Head of Domestic Affairs Bureau, arrived in his office, he found a message waiting for him to come with the Head of Foreign Affairs Bureau and the Head of Hong Kong, Macau, and Taiwan Bureau, for an urgent, unscheduled Meeting to Xin Sheng Zong's office. The Minister of State Security addressed them. "This morning, just after shaving, and as I was dressing up, I got a call from the North Korean Ambassador. Got it? The North Korean Ambassador! I have never got a call from him to date. He told me that the North Korean Television had announced in the morning that terrorists were planning to attack Guangzhou. Do any of you have any information about this?" he asked while searching their faces for some indication. Everyone looked blank.

"Get me a translator and a recording of the North Korean morning TV news. I want to watch it. Ring up your subordinates in and around Guangzhou and ask them to collect any information they may have on the subject at lightning speed, and relay it to you. If there is anything, I want to get to know it from you before it reaches the ears of our 'higher ups'. That st***d Ambassador may have rung up even our Premier, for all I know. I will probably get a call any minute now. So get on with it and get back to me. This Meeting is over!"

They left, and the Minister paced up and down in his room while his mind was busy at work. There had been some student unrests in the region in recent months that had been put down effectively. They were not terrorists. A planned *Falun Gong* rally was check-mated in Wenzhou yesterday, but that was well north of Guangzhou. Separatists were active in Xinjiang but that was a remote province, far removed from Guangzhou. Here in Beijing, there was a protest rally against unemployment a fortnight ago. It was a peaceful one, though not a desirable one. What would terrorists possibly do in Guangzhou? Bomb what? Kill or kidnap whom? Achieve what? What type of terrorists and from where? He couldn't read the tea leaves with any clarity of thought. He stopped in his tracks when there was a knock on the door.

An interpreter in the Korean language was followed by a staff member from the Technology Bureau who quickly set up the television screen in the room for viewing, and left. The playback began and the interpreter kept translating. All of a sudden, there it was!

"North Korean Intelligence has gathered that a terrorist strike is being planned on the city of Guangzhou, in neighboring China. China would do well to take note, ensure adequate protection to the city, and locate and deal with the terrorists in a befitting manner........."

It was rewound and played again. Then it was switched off and the interpreter was permitted to withdraw. Xin Sheng Zong called up Wang Jing Li, his Head of Domestic Affairs Bureau, and ordered him to promulgate a 'Security Alert' in Guangzhou and its neighboring towns, with careful scrutiny of all entering the city from neighboring Shenzen, Kowloon, and Hong Kong. He then called up the Head of the Bureau of Counter Intelligence who was in Shanghai at that moment, and apprised him of the situation. After doing this, he settled down to his daily affairs, waiting for a possible call from 'higher ups'.

His daily affairs had to wait. The many phones on his table kept ringing incessantly, and he played the role of an expert xylophone player as he deftly answered them one by one, in protocol sequence. He brooded over the possibilities of this coming week-end being a busy one with him in the office instead of going out with his family on a planned free jaunt to someone's country house in the outskirts of Beijing.

The well-oiled machinery of Chinese Intelligence and Counter Intelligence soon got into motion, and Guangzhou and its surrounds was put under intense surveillance. There was, however, one problem. No one as yet knew who they were specifically looking for.

Zheravna

The Israeli El Al Flight W64428 from Tel Aviv's Ben Gurion airport circled over Sofia airport and touched down at the appointed time on the newly built runway over the Iskar River. The bi-weekly scheduled flight was three-quarters full of tourists – mostly Europeans on their return leg from their pilgrimage to the Holy Land - and some Israelis. The airport, located on a high plateau surrounded by mountains, is susceptible to frequent heavy fog. This often resulted in diversion of flights to other nearby airports in Bulgaria or even neighboring countries. This flight was lucky. The weather was fine, bright, and sunny, the visibility clear, and the scenery very picturesque.

Onboard were two young, attractive, Israeli women in their late twenties, who were travelling together on a tourist visa to Bulgaria. Both had faces and figures that would almost definitely turn heads and invite a second look. They were cheerful, and seemingly open and friendly. Just two relaxed tourists on a holiday. This time of the year visitors came in hordes, to head mainly to Sunny Beach, the main tourist attraction of Bulgaria. The luckier ones landed in Varna. The ones to make late bookings landed in Sofia. Ariella and Frieda were not heading in that direction. They were heading in the general direction of Sliven. They had their hotel bookings in a small town of Zheravna that was just twenty kilometers from Sliven. It was booked on the internet through 'booking.com'. They had even arranged with the manager of the hotel to be picked up from the airport in Sofia, and be driven down in a taxi straight to their hotel. The journey would take them a few hours and take them through some very green country-side – something they got to see in their own country only in patches. For a few Euros more, this was more convenient than going through the hassle and delays of taking the airport shuttle service, the Metro to the centre of town, and then a bus or taxi to their destination.

The accommodation they had selected for themselves was a renovated 150 year old house. It had only seven rooms. As they entered the reception desk in the foyer, they were not disappointed with their selection. The house was built in the traditional Bulgarian architectural style, but had been fitted with all modern amenities. It had a shared, fully equipped, kitchen with a self-catered bar. The room they had decided to share had wooden flooring, satellite TV, a mini bar, a safe, and free Wi-Fi. In short, it was well equipped. It also had an attached balcony where one could sit and take in the surrounding mountain scenery. They would discover later in the evening that the village centre was just a few hundred meters away, and so was the closest grocery store. A restaurant was also within visual range.

As soon as the luggage was put in the room and the concierge had withdrawn, Ariella announced under her breath, "Let's get to work".

The two women locked the door, drew the room curtains, and went about the business of searching the room and the bathroom very thoroughly for hidden cameras, microphones, and other pick-up devices. This was done with some care and efficiency, for they were not just ordinary tourists but agents of Israel's secret service – Mossad! Both Ariella and Frieda held the ranks of commander, with Ariella being the senior of the two. The aura of confidence about them was backed by their adeptness in martial arts and hand-to-hand fighting. They were also proficient in the use of knives and weapons. They could take care of themselves. They were not here on holiday but on a highly classified mission. The names and surnames on their passports were not their real names. They found nothing in the room, which was a relief.

The rest of the day was spent in Zheravna, just like tourists, sightseeing and generally enjoying what the little town had to offer. They were careful to see that they were not followed and the curious looks they occasionally got were nothing more than a passing interest in young, pretty-looking tourists. At tea time, on their way to the center of town, they picked up a *banitsa* each from the bakery just outside the residence.

"You buy the salty one filled with white cheese, and I will buy the other sweet one with an apple filling," said Ariella to Frieda. "We can go halves and share them". Kosher food was not available – they had checked with the grocery store – but when on assignments like this one, they were permitted to relax their restrictions and atone later for their misdemeanor, after getting back.

They had heard that a *banitsa* is a greasy type of pastry that is a specialty of Bulgaria, and a 'must taste'. On their way back to their room, they dined in the restaurant within sight of their hotel room.

"Please try our grilled *kebabche*. It is one of our local favorites," suggested the waiter, and they readily agreed.

When it arrived, it came with French fries and grated *sirene* cheese on top, and a dish of *shopska salata*. The whole serving was typically Bulgarian.

Taking her first bite Ariella declared, "It appears to be a distant cousin of the hot dog, but made of pork and beef." A shared bottle of *Telish* wine washed down what was a very satisfying meal.

After a restful night, they checked out early in the morning, rather wistfully, from this quaint building, and caught a bus to Sliven. There they checked into a hotel that was centrally located, had a four-star rating, and all the amenities that go along with it. With sixty rooms, it was not as exclusive as the house in Zheravna. As part of their cover, they were to spend the first day sight-seeing.

"Let's take a guided tour," suggested Ariella, peering over a tourist map.

"There is enough to see; a visit to the ancient fortress Tuida, which dates back to the second half of the 4th century AD; the museum house of Hadzhi Dimitar; museum of Textile Industry, Art Gallery "Dimitar Dobrovich", and so on". Frieda agreed and they set out.

That evening, and every evening over the next few days, they spent in the restaurant attached to the National Palace Hotel, because that was where their work would begin and because that was where they expected to accost their 'contact'. It was the favorite haunt of Kaloyanov, the builder of condos in Sliven, and the individual with whom they had business.

Sure enough, they ran into him, or rather he approached them, for they were very noticeable. They met over three successive evenings. Kaloyanov's intentions were far from what the girls were looking for. They indulged in light flirtations over the first two evenings. Kaloyanov wanted to move faster but the girls were resisting in a manner that suggested they would eventually capitulate. So he played the game at their pace with visions of a *ménage a trois* session as the final reward. On the third evening, Ariella decided it was time to act and came straight to the point.

"We are not who you think we are," she began in a low voice. Looking him straight in the eye, she continued, "We have information from Chechen separatists that you have recently acquired something from them that we are interested in."

The blood drained from Kaloyanov's face, and his legs turned to jelly. Fortunately, he was seated or else his knees would have buckled, bringing his heavy frame to the ground. "I don't know what you are talking about," he stuttered.

"We know what we are talking about, and we also know that you have more than what we are asking you for, from old Soviet ammunition dumps," revealed Frieda.

"Who are you?" he asked in a hoarse voice.

"Never mind who we are! We would like to make a deal with you. If you cooperate, we shall give you a good price for the items you bought off the Chechens. You will have to deliver them in Varna in a place we shall indicate. After that you will not see us again, and as far as we are concerned, the matter will be finished between us," said Ariella.

There was a long silence as Kaloyanov weighed his options. He decided to go along with them. A deal was struck from which Kaloyanov got a very good bargain. The purchase and delivery of a certain consignment was to be made in Varna. Under the circumstances, he was only too glad to get the items off his hands. Kalyanov was to hand over the consignment in Varna to someone. The girls would lead him to that someone after he had collected and brought it to town. It suited him fine. The day after striking the deal, both Ariella and Frieda left Sliven, for Varna. They had more work to do there. So did Kaloyanov; but this time he would not be visiting his mother. It was back to the farm for him; not to deliver for stowage, but to collect and transport to a mutually agreed place on receipt of details from the girls.

Israeli tourists, my foot! Who were these girls, he wondered? Going over his entire conversation with them over three evenings, he realized they had revealed nothing – or nothing they had said could be linked to their profession or whoever they worked for. I must be getting rusty he rued. Now there was nothing left but for him to get it over with as quickly as possible, and put it behind him.

The Arduous Marathon

Abduweli, Yusup, and Ehmet arrived in Istanbul after a two-week long journey of 6,500 km from Islamabad, through Balochistan and Tehran, in a container train. Considering the route and terrain the train was required to go through, a maximum of 20 fully laden containers was the permissible limit. They had the necessary documents and had no trouble except for irregular meals, and some discomfort during the stretch between Quetta and Taftan in Pakistan. With the recent training that they had had, they were able to bear it. At Zahedan in Iran, they had a break-in-gauge, as the rail gauges were different in Pakistan and Iran. The containers were shifted from Pakistan's broad gauge rake to the Iranian standard gauge rake. A passenger train on this route had been promised but had not yet been introduced, and so these container trains accepted just a few 'hop-on' hikers to board and travel with proper documents, which the trio had. Turkish documents!

There were over 200,000 Uighur in Turkey, with a large number of them in Istanbul. The trio had no difficulty in getting boarding and lodging with their kinsman and within close proximity of one another. They had to wait two days before the ubiquitous Hafiz contacted them, emerging as it were from thin air! After the usual preliminaries, Hafiz opened up a bit. His policy was to never tell all in case a situation came where any or all were caught and tortured to squeal. In the event, the less they knew, the less they would be able to disclose, and the compromise would be minimal.

"The three of you will fly to Bangkok – yes, Bangkok again - where you will be met and given further instructions on what is required to be done. When you get there, go and live in the same place you had stayed in on your way out of Xinjiang. You have been selected by the *Turkistan Islamic Party* for a very important operation, the success of which will give a telling blow to China. You will be able to take the revenge you seek. At this point, I cannot tell you more than this. Are you ready for it?"

"How can we say whether we are ready or not when we do not know what we are required to be ready for?" asked Yusup with a confused look.

"We are ready" interposed Abduweli in a quiet but firm low voice. "You did say it would be a telling blow?" he enquired further.

"A telling blow it will be" assured Hafiz Mohammed again. "All the training that you have undergone will be brought to bear on this operation. You will do well, I know. That was why you were chosen. At the end of the operation, Allah will be very pleased with your actions against the perpetrators of crimes against the Uighur people."

"But, Xinjiang is far away from Bangkok. How can we inflict any harm on the Chinese from Bangkok?" asked Yusup again.

"I told you that at this stage I cannot tell you more. You must believe me. You will be told at the proper time. May Allah be with you! *Assalam-o-Alaikum!*" Saying this, the mysterious Hafiz Mohammed disappeared just as he had arrived.

Within the next 48 hours, the three of them were given airline tickets to travel onboard a Russian Aeroflot flight to Bangkok, with an hour's transit halt in Moscow's Sheremetyevo International Airport. The journey would take them around thirteen hours. There were shorter and quicker flights but some of them were expensive while others were overflying Syria and Iraq, considered as hot beds in which an aircraft could be shot down. The flight took off just after lunch. They got to Bangkok the following morning at breakfast time. Just as Hafiz had directed, they were required to find their way to *Khao San Road* in the downtown district of *Banglamphu*, where they had lived earlier on their outward bound trip from Xinjiang to Turkey. All that felt like it happened ages ago. There they were to wait for further instructions on what to do.

They were completely bowled over the next day, when the ubiquitous Hafiz Mohammed turned up, wearing a big grin that displayed all his front teeth. The look of astonishment and confusion in their eyes was something to be seen to be believed. In their wildest of imaginations, he was the last person they expected to meet. They were, however, glad to see him because with him around, they felt that certain sense of assurance that all was going as per whatever plan had been prepared for them.

"Yes, I know what you are thinking; I flew in by another, more direct, flight" he said. "You leave the day after tomorrow for Ho Chi Minh city" he continued, while handing them their tickets.

"Give me your Turkish passports. From now on, you will travel with these new passports," he said, while handing them each a very used looking passport. "What is this?" asked Yusup, "These look like old passports belonging to someone else?"

It was Ehmet's turn to look perplexed now. "This is not my name. It has been stamped with many entry and exit stamps by immigration officials from a number of countries."

Abduweli quietly observed, "They appear to be forged Turkish passports, and this is not in my name either." He looked at Hafiz questioningly.

"Learn to respond to your new names, as given in these passports, from now on, and do not respond when you are called by your actual names. This is just a precautionary step we are taking which will be good for you." Hafiz continued, "This time I shall not be there to meet you. It will be someone else, and he will give you all the information about your operation."

He stopped halfway as he was leaving and said, "There is one more thing. From now on, you must ensure that you do not do anything or go anywhere where you will be prominent or noticeable. Avoid altercations. The lesser the chances of people registering your faces in their minds, the safer it will be. Remember what you were told back in Pakistan on how you must remain concealed? Follow those instructions. Avoid carrying revealing documents and pieces of paper on your person as far as possible. Do not store incriminating information in your mobile handsets. Do not hang around together in open public spaces together for too long. May Allah be with you! *Assalam-o-Alaikum*!"

"*Wa Alaikum Assalam*" they responded. He stepped out and vanished once again.

The trio had been travelling extensively during the last three weeks or so and sorely needed time to get over jet lag and to recoup. So they just ate and slept during their stop-over in Bangkok. Rejuvenated, they boarded the Vietnam Airlines flight to Ho Chi Minh City, on which they were booked. There was no trouble with the forged passports.

Transportation

At high tide, a fully laden 40,000 metric tonner bulk carrier – the '*Bardash*' – belonging to *Bulgar Shipping Company*, cast off from the port of Varna West and left harbor, her destination – Singapore, and on to Haiphong. In her five cargo holds, she was separately carrying urea, soda ash (crude sodium carbonate), and fertilizers. Varna was one of the cheapest handling ports for such goods out of Europe. The ship was to return with rice as per the barter agreement between Bulgaria and Viet Nam. Although a vessel owned by a Bulgarian shipping company, she was flying the flag of Malta, where she was registered as a newly built ship just a few months ago. This was her maiden voyage with cargo. The Master of the ship, Captain Grozdan, had twenty five years of experience at sea in various capacities starting from a Second Officer when he was just twenty five years old. The Chief Officer, Amram Danielov, had ten years of experience at sea. The two of them were sailing together for the first time, and that too, on a brand new ship.

They were poles apart; these two. While the Captain was a seasoned, sedate, temperate, man who was quiet, yet firm when he wanted to be, the Chief Officer was a handsome, hot-headed, loud man who could swear in three languages with some fluency. Both were professionally very competent, and knew their jobs thoroughly. Both of them were Bulgarians, but from different cities. Both lived onboard most of the time. The Captain had lost his wife some years ago under tragic circumstances. They had no children. Alone in this world, without family, he decided he would spend the rest of his life at sea as long as his health would permit him. The Chief Officer was a bachelor. He was also a Jew.

The ship had come to Varna from Malta and berthed alongside for five days and five nights. That period had its own share of quiet excitement. Chief Officer Amram spent two of those nights in Sunny Beach, squandering his earnings with gay abandon. He did not allow his private life from affecting his work, for he was a conscientious sailor. Loading cargo was his responsibility, and he ensured that his work did not suffer during his short escapades.

While in Sunny Beach, Chief Officer Amram had met two Jewish women in one of the bars. Ariella and Frieda were not there by chance. In Varna, they had discreetly checked on ships heading for South East Asia and zeroed in on the *Bardash*. They had prior information about a ship with a Jewish Chief Officer onboard that was due to sail for Singapore and Haiphong soon. It was while they were approaching the ship one evening that they saw the Chief Officer leave the ship and drive off. They tailed him to Sunny Beach. The rest was a piece of cake. The wine was good and so was the ambiance. To Amram, the evening showed promise; but not for long.

Even while they were seemingly getting along well, the girls suddenly and briefly got into a huddle and whispered things to each other out of the Chief Officer's earshot. Then they both turned towards the man in front of them and stared at him intently. Sensing the change in the girls, Amram asked them what was the matter? He was startled by what followed.

"I have something important to say to you, and will come straight to the point" said Frieda as she leaned across the table towards him. "We are from Israel and we work for Mossad. You have been selected to do a small favor for our organization," she whispered to an astonished and shaken Amram. "We want you to carry a small consignment onboard your ship for delivery in Haiphong. You will be contacted once you enter Haiphong harbor, and be relieved of the consignment. This will be your contribution to Mossad under the '*sayanim*' arrangements. You will be paid well for this task – fifty percent now after embarking the consignment onboard and the balance fifty percent in Haiphong on delivery of the consignment. Will you do it?"

Amram's initial reaction was to decline, but when he heard he would be paid handsomely for it, he reconsidered it. "How much will you pay?" he asked, and both girls knew right away that one big hurdle had just got out of their way. A sum was mentioned and his eyes widened. It was a sum he just could not walk away from. He nodded his head in assent. Now Ariella continued with the subject.

"A person will contact you in Haiphong. He will find you. He will come to you and say - the *Passover falls due next month*. That will confirm that you have the right person to whom you must hand over the consignment, and from whom you will collect the balance fifty percent payment. Now, listen to me very carefully; no member of the crew, including the Captain, is to know that you have embarked the consignment. They must not know where it is stowed onboard either. This you must ensure. That is the first condition you must fulfill. Secondly, you are not to open the consignment under any conditions whatsoever. There will be no payment at the other end if it is found that the seal has been tampered with. There will be trouble for you if it is opened or not delivered. Do you understand?" Amram nodded his head in assent, but he didn't like this. He asked, "How is the consignment coming to me? If you want no one to know, no one must see it coming on board either. How big is it? Will the contents be safe to stow onboard?"

Frieda replied, "The delivery will be made tomorrow, after sunset, under cover of darkness. It will be delivered in a sealed box, and so be in a safe condition to handle. It is not an explosive, if that is what you are worried about. The box can be easily carried by a man of your stature." The three of them agreed on a time and collection point in the port, not far from where the ship was berthed. They parted company, with the girls returning to Varna, and Amram following half an hour later after imbibing some strong spirits and brooding over how he had been conned so easily.

The following evening, Kaloyanov removed the box from the farm-house of his trusted friends, and brought it to the port limits at the appointed hour. The girls met him there, and guided Kaloyanov to Amram waiting outside the port, at the appointed place. In the dimly lit rendezvous point, neither of them could see the other clearly to put a face on each other. The box changed hands under cover of darkness. It was the same one Kaloyanov had loaded in his car and brought to Varna just a few weeks earlier. The box was then taken onboard by the Chief Officer. No one saw it come onboard or learn where it was stored. Chief Officer Amram received his first part of the payment. The amount was very, very, substantial.

The *Bardash* sailed out from Varna with the next high tide and settled on a south-south-easterly course, heading for Istanbul to cross the Bosporus, exit the Black Sea, and enter the Sea of Marmara. The 6,800 nautical miles to Singapore through the Suez Canal had begun, which, at an average economical speed of 12 knots would take her not more than 24 days.

Their task completed, Ariella and Frieda took a taxi to Sofia. They caught the Air France flight from Sofia and returned to Tel Aviv via Paris. Taking indirect routes back to where they started their journey from was a part of their standard operating procedures.

Back in New Delhi, movement of the special cargo out of Varna reached Gamaliel's ears. That was good news indeed. He was told that the entire operation was executed smoothly. His part, or rather his organization's contribution, was now over. Jimmy would be told, and what he did from now onwards was something Gamaliel did not want to know. Money could do wonders. It could also keep secrets. Kaloyanov did not know where the box was going; he would not be able to identify the two Israeli girls again; the contents of the box would not be known to anyone onboard so long as Amram did not open it. Finally, and the most important part of it all, to whom the consignment was being sent was also not known – thus far.

Jimmy received the news with some jubilation. This had gone off better than he had anticipated. The only weak link in this whole chain was Gamaliel. He had done an excellent job. However, he knew too much for Jimmy's comfort. But Jimmy already had a plan to sort that out.

Agents & Double Agents

So far so good, concluded Hafiz Mohammed, as he mulled over all that had taken place these past few months. He had waited for years and years for this opportunity. He possibly would have got a chance sooner had he not had that mishap in Afghanistan that he miraculously came out of. He had a damaged, often painful, hip to live with for the rest of his life; but without a pronounced limp.

He was glad when he was approached to help in the present plot by a complete, Thai, stranger during one of his earlier visits to Bangkok some months ago. The Thai had not revealed his true identity of course, but Hafiz had suspected he was from some Intelligence organization. He had disclosed that he was in Thailand on holiday to meet his kith and kin but had settled in Ho Chi Minh City where he had a business of small proportions that paid him well. Probably a cover thought Hafiz. The stranger was from the 'opposite' camp, but was informed that Hafiz was a reliable agent. Hafiz had been playing this double role successfully so far. The funds he got from the ISIS to recruit personnel for training enabled him to move all over the world. It also gave him the license to move about freely. The fruits of his recruitment drives were so effective that nobody in their wildest dreams would have considered him to be playing a double role. His 'other' role was skillfully hidden and safe so far. He did not know for whom he was directly working, or who the boss of that mysterious outfit was, but he suspected that he was somewhere in or close to Istanbul. From time to time, in different parts of the world, he would be contacted by different people each time. The only way of recognition he had was through the codes and confirmatory words they used. That role also brought him money he could well do with. Judicious use of radio and dissemination of fake reports with clever stories prevented any suspicion falling on him from either side.

Hafiz, like Abduweli, had only one ambition in life, and that was to repeatedly and effectively hit the Chinese hard for having overrun his state of East Turkestan and killed thousands of his brethren. He was leading his life in exile from a homeland he missed very dearly. These last many years he had been working for the *Lashkar-e-Taiba*, the *ISIS*, and the *Turkistan Islamic Party*. That did not take him anywhere near getting to his goal. But it did give him comprehensive training, a toehold in these organizations, a lot of information on key *Taliban* and *Al Qaeda* leaders, as well as access to the brains of their top men. This enabled him to give human intelligence of value about important people to the 'other' side.

The Thai stranger had asked him to position two to three well-trained and motivated volunteers in Ho Chi Minh City, for an assault on some sensitive structures on the Chinese Island of Hainan. The stranger would receive them in Ho Chi Minh City and take them further. Hafiz had informed him at that time that he would need a few months to train them before handing them over, and this was agreed to. He continued to keep in touch with Hafiz over the phone at various stages, to be sure that the latter was on the job, and that all was going as per plan. He always got through to him despite Hafiz frequently changing SIM cards and mobiles handsets to cover his tracks. They had worked out an alternate system between the two of them. The last call to him was when he arrived in Bangkok after ensuring that his trio had boarded the flight from Turkey, and would follow.

It was Hafiz who thought of selecting candidates from the Uighur tribe. When he came to learn that Abduweli, the son of Abdul Haq al Turkistani had joined the *Turkistan Islamic Party* and was on his way out from Xinjiang, he tracked him down and intercepted him in Bangkok. Abduweli was a God-send, and the opportunity he was waiting for had come at last. The other two were bonus.

Now, after all that rigorous training in Pakistan, the three Uighur separatists were ready and sufficiently motivated to hit the Chinese at any time, at any place, and in any way. Hafiz was an excited man now. After handing over the volunteers and withdrawing to Turkey before the strike was launched, he would be safe to continue with his double role; till the next opportunity came his way.

There was one more loose string he had to tie up, and that was what had brought him to Ho Chi Minh City. He would have to meet up with his contact and make payment for a seized Chinese fishing vessel that was being got ready for the assault team. This money had come from the *Turkistan Islamic Party* through Istanbul. It had to be a Chinese fishing vessel because those vessels were vastly different from the Vietnamese fishing vessels. The latter variety could be easily differentiated and were often seized by the Chinese when they fished too close to Chinese territory. In fact, they were either seized or sunk when found by the Chinese anywhere near their islands or their shore line.

Not far from the City Hall - a magnificent building from the French colonial days - was the hotel in which Hafiz was staying. The hotel itself, and its surrounds, had faint traces of a colonial air about them. His room was furnished with rattan furniture of a very high quality - a reminder of the French era of slow, high, comfortable living. A walking distance away from the resplendent City Hall was the even more spectacular *Ben Thanh Market*. Hafiz headed for his appointment with his Thai contact in this market where the Thai had a shop of his own. He opted to walk down *Le Thanh Ton* despite his physical handicap, just to take in the air of a city that had gaiety and a sense of lightness written all across it, both by day and night. In sharp contrast, Hanoi and other North Vietnamese cities had a dull sober look about them that he abhorred. Ho Chi Minh City had been strongly influenced by American troop presence during the Vietnam War, when it was named Saigon. Paeans have been written in song and verse about this beautiful city under its old name.

The two met. Money changed hands. Hafiz informed his counterpart as to where the trio would be staying. He gave him a thorough briefing about the trio. He also instructed him as to where and when the Chinese fishing trawler was to be placed, and with whom. His job done, Hafiz Mohammed wound up his operations and checked out of his hotel. Posing as a tourist, with a camera in hand, he hired a car and headed for Haiphong. The road journey took two days. He had some very important work to do there.

The Voyage

The *Bardash* had emerged from the Sea of Marmara, transited through the Aegean Sea into the eastern part of the Mediterranean Sea, sailed past Port Said and entered the Red Sea through the Suez Canal. It took fourteen hours to transit the Suez Canal alone despite its widening not so long ago. Ships moved in convoys up and down the one-way canal. A desert storm converted blue skies into one big orange cloud all around the ship for a couple of hours. That was after entering the Red Sea. It was now time to confront the next problem – that of pirates, after crossing the southern exit of the Red Sea entrance. In 2010 a Bulgarian ship, *Panega*, with a crew of 15 was hijacked. That was the first Bulgarian ship to fall prey. Captain Grozdan and Chief Officer Amram Danielov prepared *Bardash* for warding off attacks by pirates.

"Chief! Issue weapons and ammunition to our earmarked marksmen! We are entering the Gulf of Aden. Uncover the dummy guns so that they are visible" said the Captain of the ship, and the Chief Officer responded.

Dummy guns were positioned in prominently visible positions on both sides of the ship, and on the bridge. They had canvas coverings that could be taken off swiftly and would not fly off in the breeze. These would be manned by personnel from the crew in bullet-proof jackets and helmets when required. Actual weapons were also positioned and manned between the dummies for use in emergency. Live ammunition was stored in a sealed compartment with the keys in Chief Officer Amram Danielov's possession. The 'consignment' he was carrying to Haiphong was also concealed in this compartment to which no one else had access. He ensured that it was concealed in such a manner that it would not be readily noticed when the compartment was opened for issue or return of ammunition.

Somali pirates were on the rampage in the Gulf of Aden and its approaches from the North Arabian Sea. They were playing havoc with shipping for years, seizing ships and taking live hostages who would be released in exchange for heavy ransom. The pirates claim they were doing this to get compensation for illegal fishing and dumping of toxic waste by ships in their waters, thereby depriving Somali fishermen of their livelihood. There were thousands of them operating. To neutralize them, navies of various countries formed a 'coalition force' that patrolled the waters 24/7. The area they covered was vast and equivalent to about a quarter of the size of the African continent. Anywhere up to twenty five warships formed a part of this coalition force at any one time. This drastically brought down the number of 'incidents' between pirates, merchant ships, and private yachts in recent years. But there had been occasions when transiting merchant ships did not find timely help coming their way to ward off an attack. So, lately many merchantmen had been resorting to carrying arms. *Bardash* was a new ship on her maiden voyage. The owners did not want to risk her getting into the hands of the pirates and had hence told the Master to carry arms for self protection. The decision was a wise one.

Having crossed the Gulf of Aden without incident, the arms and ammunition were returned to the compartment and locked up by the Chief Officer. Both during issue and recovery of arms and ammunition, he had not allowed any of the crew members to loiter around in the compartment long enough to sight his concealed 'consignment'. The crew reverted to their normal sea routine, and Captain Grozdan heaved a sigh of relief. But the relief was short-lived. *Bardash* had reached a position west of the Lakshadweep Islands, about 600 nautical miles west of the Indian Coast in the Arabian Sea, when pirates struck!

The First Officer was on watch on the bridge when he 'sighted' one medium sized and two small contacts heading towards the ship on his radar screen. "Captain, Sir," he called over the phone, "I think we have pirates showing an interest in our ship. There is one large contact that appears to be the mother ship hovering around some distance away, and two smaller contacts that are closing us at some speed. You are requested to come up to the bridge." The Captain replied, "On my way; get Chief to issue weapons and ammunition to our crew immediately." In a trice, the Captain was on the bridge. One look through his binoculars and he asked the radio operator to send off distress signals giving their present position on the chart.

Soon two skiffs were sighted, approaching them at high speed. The two split up, and one went on one side and the other to the other side of the ship. They had two persons each on their upper decks and they were carrying weapons. Through the side windows, barrels of guns were also visible that showed that there were some more of them armed and concealed in the covered cabin. Captain Grozdan ordered his Second Officer to stand on the Bridge and video tape both the skiffs and their movements from a safe position. On the horizon, abeam of the *Bardash*, the mother vessel could be seen. She was maintaining her distance from the Bulgarian merchant vessel. The skiffs slowed down and maintained a parallel course on either side. They appeared to be hesitating. Perhaps they had seen the weapons prominently displayed on the upper deck of the ship with a man behind each weapon. Suddenly, an Indian Coast Guard aircraft appeared from the direction of the Lakshadweep Islands. The two skiffs altered Course and high-tailed it straight to the mother vessel. The skiffs were hoisted onboard the pirate mother vessel quickly. She moved away westwards with a circling aircraft over them for company. The crew onboard *Bardash* heaved a sigh of relief and the ship proceeded on course, heading for the southern tip of Sri Lanka. They believed that by arming themselves, they had bought those few precious minutes of hesitation on the part of the pirates, which was sufficient for the Indian Coast Guard aircraft to arrive on the scene. The mother vessel was later apprehended by Indian Naval ships. Some pirates were killed, some captured, and some hostages onboard were rescued.

There was no further excitement till the *Bardash* rounded the southern tip of Sri Lanka and ran eastwards across the Bay of Bengal. While nearing the Nicobar Islands, and about 80 nautical miles short of it, an Indian Naval maritime patrol aircraft appeared as if from nowhere and inquisitively circled the ship. It then flew away in a northerly direction. An hour later, two Indian Naval warships approached her from northwards and circled her. The *Bardash* dipped her ensign like all other merchantmen dip their ensigns to warships all over the world. She got an immediate response from the nearer one of the two who reciprocated. The two of them then went away, one to a position 5 nautical miles to the starboard bow of *Bardash* and the other 5 miles to the port quarter of her. There they remained till the ship got to the approaches to the Strait of Malacca. Captain Grozdan thought little of it and dismissed it as an action by a navy keeping a watchful eye over their waters. He did not think they were particularly interested in his ship in any way.

Indonesian pirates were expected at the entrance to the Malacca Strait and Captain Grozdan again gave the order to arm personnel and position them in vantage points again. He had planned the ship's passage in such a way that both the Gulf of Aden and the Malacca Strait would be transited by *Bardash* by day.

The Malacca Strait is busy with shipping throughout the year. Around forty percent of all world trade and oil from the gulf countries is transported through it to South East Asia and the Far East. In navigational terms, it is a narrow sea-way full of islets, making it a haven for pirates who would launch surprise attacks. Like in the Gulf of Aden, here too, the neighboring states have got together to suppress piracy and have succeeded to a great extent. Nevertheless, a threat to passing merchant ships exists since it has not been completely exterminated. Once again, *Bardash* prepared herself for a surprise attack, but was not targeted. The transit was peaceful, and she entered Singapore harbor to unload and load freight. Being a fast moving and efficient port, she was out on the second day, and on her way in a northerly direction on a route between the Gulf of Thailand and the South China Sea. Hugging the eastern seaboard of Vietnam, she arrived in the comparatively primitive port of Haiphong in the Gulf of Tonkin exactly one month after leaving Varna. As no other cargo ship of her tonnage was in harbor at that moment, she was given an alongside berth immediately so as to discharge her consignment. This kept the Chief Officer busy the whole night and through much of the second day.

On the evening of the second day after arrival, just after he had stepped out of his ship and was on his way out of the docks, Chief Officer Amram Danielov was accosted by a middle-aged man. He sported a clean cut beard supported by a mop of curly hair on his head with the central portion bald and devoid of any growth. Only those over six feet tall could see the bald patch. He was not a Vietnamese. That was obvious. He was fair skinned with grayish blue eyes, and looked more like an east European or a Turk.

"I believe I have some payments to make to you, and, in return, you have something to hand over to me," said the stranger without introducing himself.

"Who are you?" asked the wary Chief Officer. "Please identify yourself" he continued.

"That won't be necessary. *The Passover falls due next month*" he replied. For a moment Amram Danielov did not see the connection between the two sentences. Then suddenly, he remembered! It was the password! He had almost forgotten it.

It was not quite dark, and the Chief Officer did not want to hand over the box when the visibility was good. So he asked the man to wait till 10:00pm, by when he would return. He could take it then. The man agreed and withdrew. Amram Danielov went ashore to taste the local brew and cuisine. Alone! A few local girls approached him and promised him a good time in exchange for "Dollahs". He cursed his luck. He promised to return to them at 11:00pm, and returned to the ship.

The consignment and money changed hands. In a state of euphoria, Amram went back to the girls, and had one big celebration, but not before stowing most of his 'earnings' safely, in his cabin onboard!

Hafiz Mohammed left in a waiting car with the consignment. He moved fast to a laboratory in a quiet part of town where he met two persons to whom he handed over the consignment. Some money was also handed over, and Hafiz departed by road from the city of Haiphong that same night. He was not very comfortable in Haiphong and wanted to get out fast. He headed back to Ho Chi Minh City and caught the next flight to Bangkok. From there he headed for Indonesia, again to recruit more volunteers to train and fight for 'the common cause' in Syria and Iraq. He would get back to Haiphong in a few days, in time to finally brief the 'trio', in accordance with instructions received from the 'other side'. He also wanted to give them a final boost before they went on their way.

Ho Chi Minh City

Stepping out into the main foyer of the Tan Son Nhat International Airport of Ho Chi Minh city after completing immigration formalities, Abduweli, Yusup, and Ehmet found a man approaching them purposefully. They locked eyes and when he was within audible range he looked at all three of them and called out to Abduweli by the new name in his passport. Contact was established. They shook hands and he led them out to a waiting van across the road in the parking slot. Not a word was spoken as they moved out of the parking area and headed into town some 6 km away. At the outskirts of the city itself, they slipped into noisy traffic. The driver moved away from the main road and turned off into a side road. Once on a quieter road, the driver of the vehicle spoke slowly and deliberately in Pashtu, but with a bad accent.

"I no speak Pashtu well. We have interpreter. We speak then" and he lapsed into silence once again, concentrating and weaving his way past hordes of two wheelers and rickshaws on either side of the road, all moving in whichever direction or side they found most convenient, with no concern for any traffic rules. The trio looked at each other and then decided to maintain silence and absorb the city sights. Another half an hour and they were taken down a very heavily populated narrow street till the van could go no further. They stopped, got off, and stepped out, following the driver on foot. All the signboards were in the local language and the trio could not make out a thing! To Abduweli, it appeared as if they were in some downtown part of the city. Five minutes later, they were led through a shabby door into a low roofed room where they found three men waiting. The interpreter got up and addressed them in Pashtu.

"Good Day! The person who brought you from the airport in his van is Gan. He is a Thai by birth but lives here. I am your interpreter and my name is Duc. This man on my right is Hai, and the one on my left is Thanh. Welcome to Ho Chi Minh City! We hope you had a pleasant journey and are not too tired. We now have some briefing and then we will show you to your accommodation. I am sorry, the accommodation may not meet your standards, but you must remember that Vietnam is not a rich country, and so please bear with us." They all shook hands and the trio introduced themselves by their newly inherited names. Tea was served in the traditional Vietnamese style.

Gan then got up and addressed them in the local language. Sentence by sentence the interpreter translated what was being said.

"You three have been chosen to carry out some training here on specific equipment and, on completion, move on to Haiphong where you will get further training on some other subjects. My role in this is to give you the training here. Hai and Thanh will be your instructors. They will work with you through interpreter Duc, here. First, I have been instructed to get a make-up artist to make you look like Chinese fishermen. Then, we will educate you on basic customs and traditions of Vietnamese and Chinese persons. We shall also conduct basic classes for you to speak in mandarin. Some of you may have learnt the language in your homes already, but we will teach you the colloquial mandarin as spoken in South China. Do you have any questions?"

Interpreter! Vietnamese and Chinese customs! Made to live as Chinese fishermen! There was bewilderment in the minds of the trio who were wondering where they had landed up, and whether all this was leading up to what they really wanted to do. Where was Hafiz? Did he know what they were being put through?

"How long is the training here and in that next place you spoke about going to be? And after that, what are we supposed to do?" asked Yusup.

"Your training here will be for a week. We will complete all that we have been told to teach you in this time. We have no idea what training you are going to undertake in Haiphong, and neither do we know what the duration of that training is going to be. Before you ask, we do not know what you are going to do after all the training has been completed. That is not in our interest. But the one who sent you here from Bangkok asked me to tell you that the time to fulfill your dreams is drawing near," said Gan with a wry smile.

"Now, please hand over your passports. We have new ones for you with your new Chinese names. They are made well after a lot of effort by experts. Even the Chinese authorities will not be able to make out that they are not originals. These are the documents Chinese fishermen carry with them."

The disguise to look like Chinese fishermen was deftly done. It was touched up daily, first thing in the morning. During the day, classes were held in the South Chinese mandarin dialect, and basic Vietnamese language. The mandarin classes were not too difficult, as a parallel could be drawn to the mandarin taught to them in Xinjiang in their schools. They had learnt Pashtu during training in Pakistan; the Vietnamese language was, however, very different and difficult for all three to assimilate. They bravely plodded on. During daylight hours they were not permitted to step out in the open; they were confined indoors. After sunset, when darkness had set in, they were taken up the Saigon river to a less populated place where they were given lessons in swimming, treading water, and practice in inflating and deflating rubber dinghies in total darkness, without even a torch. Everything was conducted professionally and away from prying eyes.

Once the training was over, they were taken by road to Haiphong, covering a distance of approximately 1800 km over two days. In the vehicle, they had Gan and Duc for company till they arrived in Haiphong and were accommodated in a cheap tourist hotel named Dong Vinh Hotel. After they had checked into prepaid adjacent rooms, they were fed and were left with food packets for further repasts, as they were not expected to converse with the staff. Both Gan and Duc bade them farewell and left, not to be seen again. So here they were – three Chinese looking Uyghur, with Chinese names, unable to converse in the local language and posing as tourists, waiting for the next lot to get in touch with them. In his youth, Abduweli had often dreamt of touring countries and seeing the world. The first part of his dream had been more than fulfilled these past few months, but not in the way he had imagined. The second part also remained largely unfulfilled. Tired after two hectic days of travelling, they hit the bed hard and were asleep in moments.

On the day of their departure, the local papers contained a paragraph that told the story of a body of a man being fished out of the river, and that his identity had been established. He was a make-up artist by profession.

Puppets & Puppeteers

News of the arrival of the consignment and the executors in Vietnam reached Jimmy, and he was on top of the world. He wanted to share his joy with someone. This had gone off better than he had anticipated. However, he knew that the most difficult part was yet to come. During his routine briefings in South Block (corridors of power in New Delhi) he would meet the National Security Advisor often, and the Prime Minister, during special meetings. There was no talk on this subject. One or the other would raise their eyebrows while looking at Jimmy and he would nod his head very slightly. That was all. They talked of other matters of national importance. The only weak link in this whole chain was Gamaliel. He knew just that little too much for Jimmy's comfort. It was now time to neutralize that threat.

Jimmy Ahuja drove out of New Delhi towards the city of Meerut late one night. There were many routes, but he took the 90 km long controlled-access expressway connecting the two cities via Dasna in Ghaziabad. He dismissed his chauffer and drove his car by himself. He had the CIA gadget on his person, the one handed over to him at CIA Headquarters in Langley during his visit there many months ago. The codes for communication and the instructions for its use, was also on his person. While on the Highway, he called up the Assistant to the Director for Foreign Intelligence Relations, Paul Courtney, in CIA Headquarters. He came on line.

"Just wanted some help" said Jimmy without any introductions. "So far, things are going well. We have made a lot of progress. I have used the assistance of one Gamaliel in the Israeli embassy here in Delhi for a small portion of the activities. He is from Mossad. He does not know too much, but still, I want him taken care of. Can you help?"

"We will see what we can do" drawled the voice at the other end and the coded communications went dead. Jimmy drove on for a little while and entered the township of Muradnagar where he did a few twists and turns, and then drove back to New Delhi.

A few days later, Gamaliel met Al Turner from the US Embassy. The meeting did not go well. Al Turner read the riot act to Gamaliel, drawing attention to his dark past that the latter, in his wildest dreams, could not have believed anyone knew. Some of them were, regrettably, true and from his early marriage days. Others were distortions of some of the activities he had carried out as a member of Mossad. The distorted versions, for which he had no alibi for himself, Gamaliel knew, would get him into serious trouble if brought out in the public domain. He was advised to keep silent about his help to Jimmy Ahuja. Should he open his mouth, he would be incriminated with facts and planted information, and land himself in trouble. Blackmail! Possibly a bump off! Gamaliel's silence was bought. He cursed the Americans. He cursed Jimmy. He cursed Glenfiddich! But beyond that he had only himself to curse. So that was it! Jimmy had CIA backing! The sly fox! All this in return for having skillfully spun a yarn to his superiors that got them going on the project of getting the consignment through the girls onboard the *Bardash,* without an 'Indian hand' being suspected of being involved; and as a favor to Jimmy whom he had got to like! He learned another lesson that day that he was not likely to ever forget as long as he lived. He now was looking forward to the impending transfer he was expecting. The routine meetings between Jimmy and Gamaliel were discontinued.

Back in office the next morning, Jimmy's mind was working overtime. He went over every bit of the plans, conversation between him and others on the subject, work executed so far, and work planned ahead. His mind flipped back and forth over the events. Had there been any slip-ups or oversight? Can events be traced back to the countries and those that should be concealed? Were there any weak links to be tied up – like the one he had just taken care of? The Thai contact in Ho Chi Minh City had done well. He could never reveal who he had been working for because all his orders were coming from Istanbul from someone whose voice he recognized but whom he had never met. This was the same contact he received all his orders from and made all his reports to. In any case, to survive in a communist country, one advisedly kept one's mouth shut. Jimmy hadn't dealt with him directly but through a Uighur contact. He was almost, but not fully, convinced that things were proceeding smoothly. More than once he had cursed himself for putting his noose in the neck and courting trouble – and all for what? No one would ever learn about his involvement in this operation to congratulate him after the job was done. So there would be no bouquets. Would the Prime Minister reward him – with a citation? Unlikely! He did not even dare to put it in his memoirs – if he ever wrote one. He would have to live with that for the rest of his life. Unsung! He concluded that in this world of cloak and dagger that he lived in, all that he was getting or going to get was one hell of a kick out of doing it, with a bigger kick at the end; if all went well. It was best not to think about the other kick he would get if things went wrong.

With continued and utmost secrecy, he now had to get the executers to prepare the ordnance, take it across, and carry out the task. He had arranged for the preparation to be conducted in a private laboratory in Haiphong. This was no ordinary laboratory. It had one science graduate and another with a doctorate trained in the United States, and now engaged in pure research for their country. Both had lost close family members during the Sino-Vietnam 1979 war, and hated the Chinese and their country. They had quietly agreed to help. He recalled how the Mumbai attack in 2008 was launched from seaward. He was planning to do something similar. It had worked then. It should work now. A captured Chinese trawler, now in Haiphong, was available for the purpose. The Uighur trio would be onboard.

Chinese coast guard and Intelligence had to be countered, and then it should be easier thereafter.

The winds in Hainan would have to be favorable for the operation to be effective. The winds were strong between October and February. Commencing in October, the winds were from south or south-west. It would alter slowly but steadily, and end up from northwards by February. During most of the rest of the year, the winds were unreliable and interspersed, often, by occasional typhoons. Steady westerly winds blew in August around Dongfang and Haiwei, on the west coast of Hainan. This was around 200 miles from Haiphong. This was ideal for his plans. So, August was the month he would launch his attack. There was time. He shuddered with excitement to think of what was likely to happen after the event. Certainly, he would not like to be around anywhere there.

There was another matter. He had been in touch with the head of the General Department of Military Intelligence of Vietnam for quite some time now. He was an army officer and many years ago, they had done a Course together in the Infantry School in Mhow, in Madhya Pradesh, India. It was important that he kept the Vietnamese in the loop since their shores were being used. The 'colleague' worked directly under their Ministry of Defense (TC2). The Director of TC2 was also an army officer, of the rank of a Lieutenant General, who reported directly to The Party and the President. Jimmy had sought the assistance of the head of the General Department of Military Intelligence for tacit support for the whole operation. For this, he had gone to neutral territory, to Bangkok, to meet him on two occasions. He finally got it! This, he felt, was the biggest breakthrough he had achieved, and that too at his level without any official government to government contact whatsoever! It made things much easier to cover up tracks after the event, and prevent attribution of blame to anyone other than the Uighur separatists.

Now for the final phase, thought Jimmy to himself, dismissing Murphy's Law and any other Law one could think of that might hinder the progress. Instinct told him that he would succeed from the day he got the clearance from the Vietnamese, and learnt that the weapons and team had arrived at their pre-assault positions.

A fortnight after Jimmy's drive down to Meerut, the newspapers carried a front page news item that read that an Israeli diplomat had committed suicide in his residence. The usual condolences were sent by the External Affairs Ministry to the Israeli Embassy, and representatives lined up at the airport when the body and the family boarded a plane to Ben Gurion airport in Tel Aviv. Jimmy did not visit the family to pay condolences. He could not bring himself to do it.

Haiphong

Three local men, in normal worker's overalls, came to Dong Vinh Hotel the following morning and knocked on one of the two rooms the trio had been accommodated in. Abduweli was alone in that room; Yusup and Ehmet were together in the room next door. Survival instincts and training made Abduweli cautious and he muffled his voice and spoke through the door in indistinct Vietnamese, after the second knock. A voice answered in Pashtu, and requested him to open the door. Thinking it was Duc, the interpreter from Ho Chi Minh City he lowered his guard and peeped through the magic eye, half expecting a bullet to hit his eye. Three strangers were standing in front of his door. This time he asked them what they wanted in Pashtu, and one of them replied that they knew who he was, that they were friends, and to open the door. Clutching a knife he had on his person, ready to strike, Abduweli cautiously opened the door. The three men just stood there, and the man who had spoken earlier asked him to put away the unseen knife and to step aside so that they could come in. Hesitantly, Abduweli complied, and the three men entered. They then asked Abduweli to call his two friends from next door into the room. An exchange of coded knocks next door and Yusup and Ehmet stepped out of their room and entered Abduweli's room. They were about to attack the three strangers when Abduweli held them back and stated they were friends. A similar procedure to the one in Ho Chi Minh City followed by way of introductions. The interpreter spoke first.

"My name is Hieu. I am your interpreter. I do not speak your language or Pashtu too well, but we will manage," he grinned, flashing a generous row of yellow buck-toothed teeth.

"My comrades here are Dat and Hoang," he continued, pointing out to each of them in turn. "They will be giving you some training that you will find useful for your next operations. We will not discuss it here. Please clear your rooms and go out from the front lobby of the hotel. We will follow a few minutes later. Across the road you will find a minibus parked. It is white with a yellow star on the side door. The rear door is badly dented. Cross the road, go to the other side of the bus and wait for us where the hotel staff cannot see you. Quickly now! We must not waste time."

The trio complied. By now they were just going along with everything they were being confronted with, in the hope and trust that all these were the doings of Hafiz. They had no other choice. They were totally out of their depths in strange surroundings. The end goal kept them going.

The three Vietnamese soon joined them and they got into the minibus. One of them, – Dat, by name – drove the vehicle. The other two were with the trio in the rear portion. Interpreter Hieu was talking. At first they found him difficult to follow. So they requested him to speak deliberately and slowly. He obliged. They gathered that they were being taken to an isolated bay on the outskirts of Haiphong where a Chinese fishing boat was positioned. They would be staying onboard. They would be familiarized with handling the boat and its fishing equipment. They would be taught how to use all the fishing boat lights and signals that the Chinese use, and how to communicate by hand signals the Chinese way. They would be given Chinese weapons, and equipment to try out and get familiar with. Dat and Hoang will also be living with them onboard the Chinese trawler for a few days. They would be making frequent visits to a laboratory in Haiphong during dark hours, for further briefing. All this was told to them while they were weaving in and out of noisy traffic, avoiding swerving two-wheelers, and through horns of different frequencies blaring constantly. Gradually, the noise and traffic receded and they found themselves out of Haiphong and on a lonely country road heading south along the coast till they finally arrived at their destination. Before them was a makeshift jetty of sorts, tied to which was their 'home'.

The six of them stepped onboard. The trio found a host of equipment already loaded. At first it looked like a fishing boat with nets, buoys, floats, pots and pans for cooking, a stove, food items, etc all plainly visible. The wheelhouse had a GPS unit. Unknown to them, it was already programmed with the landing coordinates of the destination. Night vision goggles were also hanging from a hook in the cabin. But under the bunk beds and the floorboards they were shown the arms and ammunition stored for their use. All three of them let out whoops of joy on seeing the familiar equipment.

There were three blinding hand held laser guns used by the Chinese Police Force that were not familiar. They were foldable, with trigger guard, and pistol grip. A battery pack was in the butt. They had telescopic sights. They were designed to blind sensors and personnel so that they would not be in a position to deploy their own weapons. They could even blind helicopter pilots and night vision equipment.

There were detonators, tins of powdered RDX explosives, Chinese Type 90, Type 69 and Type 59 grenades, Chinese cartridges, and other Chinese weapons.

The trio was able to recognize most of the weapons because they were trained on them in Pakistan. Two QBZ-95, 5.8mm Bull pup Assault rifles, two CS-LR3, 5.8x42mm sniper rifles, one QCW-05, 5.8mm suppressed sub machine gun, and three QSZ-92, 5.8mm pistols, were all neatly stacked in such a way that they could be removed easily and quickly.

A low whistle emanated from Ehmet's lips. There was a gleam in all their eyes. They were keenly watched for reactions by Dat, Hoang, and Hieu who appeared to be convinced that the trio was familiar with the equipment, and knew how to use each one of them, and that was a relief as it made their task easier.

Hieu then spoke, "Here in Vietnam, our fishing hamlets know each other well and can quickly recognize unfamiliar boats. That is why this Chinese boat – in an unarmed state, of course – had been parked these last few weeks in the neighboring fishing hamlets in full view for all to see, for a few days at a time. Everyone was told the truth – that it was captured from the Chinese. They will know the boat when they see it moving about. The chances of her being reported to our internal security networks by local informants therefore are slim. But when you enter Chinese waters, beware. They have the same, perhaps more strict, surveillance system. They will be quick to spot an unfamiliar boat. I wish you well."

"Where are we to go?" asked Yusuf.

"That answer is not with us. You will get it during your night visits," said Hieu as he glanced at the expressionless faces of Hoang and Dat.

They quickly got down to business. The first step was to handle the boat by day. Later they would learn to handle it at night. They were shown, and practiced, how to lower their nets in the water and how to haul them in. After that, they would learn how to repeat this at night with the flood lights on. They were taught how to handle the engine at high speeds and low speeds; how to start and stop it and maneuver the boat with the engine off, but underway. In fact, they were taught all that was to be learnt to handle the boat like competent fishermen. The following day this was repeated. In addition, they were given Chinese SIM cards and handsets with battery chargers, and Chinese fishermen's fake identity cards. That night, they were taken into town by Hieu to a certain laboratory where they were to be given their final instructions.

The calendars all over the world sequentially turned to the month of August at midnight, local time.

The Preparation

In the still of the night, in a laboratory located in a basement of an obscure looking building somewhere in Haiphong, a Professor with a doctorate in nuclear physics and his assistant, a science graduate, had assembled to prepare instruments of destruction. Anyone walking in the street, or living nearby would not have noticed anything unusual because all blinds were drawn across windows on the ground and first floors; in addition, the window panes of the ground floor windows had all been covered with black paper for months. All lights on the ground and first floors (there were only two floors) were off. The basement lights could not be seen by anyone outside the building. The doors were all locked from inside. There were no vehicles parked in or around the laboratory that night except for the few neighborhood ones that usually parked in the area every night. The duo was dressed in radio-active protective clothing.

The duo had a collection of items at hand that were easily procurable from local shops across the city without raising any undue suspicion. There were lots and lots of mantles used in gas lanterns, an equal if not more number of smoke detector alarms, aluminum foils, some charcoal, some lithium batteries, a cube of lead with a gouged out cavity on one side, a blowtorch, some cooking oil, a tin can, six glow-in-the-dark wall clocks, and a few cobalt drill bits.

"Shall we begin?" asked the Professor of his Assistant. "Yes Sir," the latter replied. "I think we have all the ingredients at hand. I have checked the items against the list." They commenced their work with minimum fuss.

First the mantles were unpacked and put in a large crucible, and blow torched to form a powder. The mantles were made from thorium; a fair quantity settled at the bottom of the crucible, and was allowed to cool. The Assistant extracted Lithium strips from the batteries, wiped them clean, and sprinkled a portion of prepared thorium powder from the crucible on the strips. The powdered strips were then wrapped in foil to form a small ball. A can of oil was then brought by the Assistant under supervision of the Professor. He immersed the wrapped up piece in the can of oil and, together, they heated up the oil to a very high temperature to form pure thorium – enough for a make-shift, mini nuclear reactor!

"In such a mini reactor, the thorium can be transmuted to uranium or plutonium, which is our objective," stated the Professor. "To do this," he continued, "the elements have to be made radio-active. How do we do this?" he asked, looking at his Assistant. "I don't know, Sir. I mean, we will need a neutron gun, wouldn't we? We don't have one" replied the Assistant, looking at his superior in a puzzled way. "So, we will now make a neutron gun. It won't be too difficult to make one," said the Professor with a smile on his lips. The two of them got down to making one! There was minimum conversation between the two as they went about what appeared to be a well thought out drill, even though they were doing this for the first time.

From the hundreds of smoke detectors, they extracted Americium which is one of the trans-uranium elements produced by beta rays decay of an isotope of plutonium. It is a good source of alpha particles. This was a tedious piece of work which took them a couple of hours. The radio-active Americium was rolled into a ball and inserted into the gouged out cavity in the lead block, and covered with aluminum sheeting. This produced subatomic particles of neutrons. The formed particles of neutrons interact with the wrapped up ball to make it radioactive.

The duo now turned their attention to the clocks. They removed the radium coated hands of the clocks and immersed them in a solvent to remove the coating. The resultant solution became a high-grade source of liquid radium for use in the make-shift mini reactor.

The silence was broken by the Professor. "Let us now mix the radium solution and the Americium from the lead block, and roll the two into a ball. After that we shall wrap the ball in foil." The two proceeded with this step, and after they had completed this bit, the Professor stepped back and announced with some satisfaction, "Now the core for the make-shift mini reactor is ready".

The next step they got busy with was to make tiny, identical sized cubes from the balance thorium in the crucible mixed with ordinary charcoal. Each one of these was then wrapped separately in their own foil covers. Once again, they checked that each small cube was of the same size as the other. These small cubes were then stacked together to form a larger cube that looked somewhat like a Rubik's cube. The larger cube was tightly wrapped all round with tape to remain bound, and in shape.

"Now we have the core, and one large cube," announced the Professor. "We need to drop the core into the center of the cube". They worked together, and the core was placed right in the center of the one large cube that they had made. This took awhile as they had to get it just right.

"Please hand me the cobalt drill bits," said the Professor, and the Assistant complied. "These will be inserted at the appropriate time to act as control rods," he muttered. The make-shift mini reactor, with the control rods inserted, was now ready to produce weapon grade plutonium! They then took a break as they had been working non-stop for quite awhile.

This was the duo's contribution to 'the effort', as a measure of revenge for their losses to the Chinese. The work was finished by 5:00 AM and they decided to get some sleep. They had enough food with them and so did not have to go out for anything. There was one more night's work left. After that, they would have some waste disposal to take care of.

The following night, the duo got onto the next project. Just a few days earlier, a Uighur had come to the lab and left a box with them. They donned their protective radioactive clothing and gingerly opened the box. "Now what do we have here?" enquired the Professor while peering into it. "It seems to me, there are five teletherapy cylinders, stacked side by side." Peering over his shoulders the Assistant chipped in, "They are all of the same dimensions – about four centimeters in diameter and three and a half centimeters in height each?" The Professor nodded his head to confirm it. Being nuclear physicists, they well knew that the outer lead body would have a protective internal shield that usually consisted of uranium metal or tungsten alloy. Inside the internal shield there would be a radioactive source material that could either be Cobalt-60, or powdered Caesium–137. They removed the cylinders from the box and placed them separately.

"Now comes a tricky part," said the Professor, looking at his Assistant. "Bring those conventional IED bombs here one by one. Be careful not to drop them. We have to modify each of them to take in one of these teletherapy cylinders apiece, for which we will have to do some minor modifications on the IED bombs." Both knew this was a very risky and dangerous job. They were sweating and nervous. Yet they knew the job had to be done. Gingerly, they worked extremely slowly on the first one. Having done one successfully, they grew in confidence and did the second one with less apprehension. Finally, well into the night, they finished all five of them. They were exhausted and took a break. Sipping a glass of water, the Professor said, "When these conventional IED bombs are detonated, they would lethally kill anyone within a radius of a couple of hundreds of yards, but equally, spread radioactive material in the air, and that would set of a catastrophic chain of reactions.

A sixth bomb was created from the weapon grade plutonium produced by the make-shift mini reactor made in the lab the previous night.

Explosions from these types of bombs could result in three reactions. Firstly, they would have to attend to the wounded and the dead who were around when the explosion takes place. Secondly, they would evoke reactions from the surviving people in the locality. While the effect on the people from radiation exposure could be limited, knowing about the presence of radioactive particles in the air could evoke a psychological impact that would invite far greater reactions. This could almost definitely result in public hysteria and large scale evacuation from the area. Evacuation, in turn, could result in the next reaction; the economy of the region taking a big hit. The clean-up procedure would of necessity be a long drawn out and very expensive affair.

The Sniffing Dragon

Xin Sheng Zong, The Minister of State Security, was disturbed to see that a certain anti China TV channel had broadcast to the world that China was secretly removing organs from arrested *Falun Gong* followers to meet the requirements of senior and important citizens, then killing them and disposing off their bodies. The report was highly exaggerated, according to him. He decided that something needs to be done to suppress the TV Company, and issued instructions to conduct a search to locate the informers and have them arrested. Such adverse publicity was bad for his nation that was on its way to becoming a super power.

He was also a little perturbed to read a vague intelligence report placed on his table which said that a terrorist attack on China was imminent. It suggested that the attack would be from seawards. That more or less ruled out dissidents from within China. Where could they come from? – South Korea? – Japan? - Taiwan? - The ASEAN nations?

There were enough problems at sea with foreign navies conducting naval exercises at China's doorsteps that were not in the interests of his nation. Just recently, Japan, the USA, and India had conducted a tri-nation exercise in the Sea of Japan. The US Navy had made taunting forays into the South China Sea – their sea - with an aircraft carrier, ships and ship-borne aircraft. Some units of the Indian Navy, exercising with the Vietnamese navy, had joined up with the US Forces. This had emboldened the Vietnamese navy who also made noises. And all this because a Chinese Coast Guard ship had sunk a few Vietnamese fishing craft that had entered Chinese fishing area, and were poaching! Such forays are likely to increase, to test Chinese reactions and responses. The decisions given in the Permanent Court of

Arbitration, in The Hague, against China and ruling in favor of Philippines' petition on ownership of islands in the South China Sea was a set-back to his country. The Chinese vice Foreign Minister had only recently stated that defense facilities were being built on islands far away from the mainland as a part of national defense and safeguarding Chinese islands and reefs, and that it should not be mistaken for actions to militarize the South China Sea. Then there was the ongoing fishing war between ASEAN trawlers and Chinese trawlers.

Xin Sheng Zong was disturbed by the reactions by the rest of the world. Did they not know that fifty one percent of all the fishing conducted worldwide was by China alone, for its own domestic consumption? The large Chinese population needed sea food to maintain good protein levels in their bodies. For this, Chinese fishing fleets were going far and wide to bring home adequate catches, and even as far as to the South Atlantic. As he and the rest of the country with him saw it, all the sea food in the South China Sea belonged to them and this should be accepted by the rest of the world. Chinese fishing trawlers respected the territorial water limits of neighboring states. Occasionally, Chinese trawlers in the Gulf of Tonkin strayed into Vietnamese territorial waters through 'errors in navigation', but were promptly chased away by the Vietnamese.

A few weeks ago, he was trapped into carrying out a massive security exercise in Guangzhou and its surrounding districts by the scare put out by the North Koreans. He had come away red-faced from that experience. There had been no threat to the city or its surrounds. Manpower, time, and money were wasted in the process. It was the North Korean Ambassador's phone call that did it. Xin Sheng Zong decided that such a fiasco would not be repeated again. The next time – if there was going to be a next time – he was going to be more sure and deliberate in his actions. He would be more careful to check the authenticity of reports before acting. He consoled himself by accepting the fact that the last exercise was a good rehearsal for such an eventuality, should it actually ever occur.

Xin Sheng Zong was to retire by the end of the year and he wanted the rest of the year to pass smoothly, without any fiascos. He also wanted to concentrate on making arrangements for his family to have a comfortable style of living after his retirement. He had to do this now, while still occupying his present post. Once he vacated his chair, no one would help him and he would be on his own. This was the pattern he had observed amongst the Chinese hierarchy. Some exceeded limits and came to grief. Most of them remained within limits and got away with it. The limits depended upon the rank and status in the government. He knew how much he could push and expect.

He could pat himself on his back for the tremendous work he had put in to produce a draft Counter Terrorism Law that was eventually included as a section in the President's 'Overall National Security Outlook'. In the coming months, he was expecting the President to suitably reward him for this. The last thing he wanted at this stage was a terrorist attack. If it happens, the element of surprise would be to the advantage of the attacker, which always and invariably exposed chinks in the counter systems in place.

He sent for Wang Jing Li, the Head of Domestic Affairs Bureau who, as always, appeared within minutes as if from nowhere.

"You know, Wang Jing Li I have this very vague report on my table about an imminent terrorist strike from seaward on our mainland. Do you know anything about it?" As anticipated, he got a negative answer.

"That last futile exercise that we carried out in Guangzhou got me into hot water with our superiors. I don't want such an incident repeated. We must be more careful and deliberate and not over react to information from outside intelligence sources that are not our own, without authenticating the information first," said the Minister. He continued,

"How are our security arrangements along our coastline?"

"The honorable Minister is fully aware that we have a very tight coastal security system that is ever alert and ready to apprehend anyone attempting to endanger our motherland" replied Wang Jing Li with a fluency that suggested that such statements came easily to him through years of practice.

"Are our Coast Guard ships equally alert?" enquired Xin Sheng Zong.

"They are performing very efficiently, Minister. Just the other day, they caught five Vietnamese trawlers fishing off *Pinyin* (Spratly Islands). They rammed and sank all of them," replied the Head of Domestic Affairs Bureau. "I am in constant touch with the Heads of Local Intelligence and Counter Intelligence; in fact our Bureaus interact with each other like a well knit team," waxed Wang Jing Li eloquently. "The Minister can rest assured that we will have no problems from seaward. If we do, we shall take care of them."

The Minister was staring intently at the map of the South China Sea on the wall on his left. Mainland China's map hung directly in front of him, and a map of the Western Pacific Region hung on the wall on his right. With a nod of his head he dismissed Wang Jing Li, who bowed and withdrew as silently as he had appeared. Left alone, he turned to his desk top computer and clicked on *Baidu* to hunt for some information from the net. He decided he would pass the buck: he would inform his superiors and leave it to them to decide what course of action to take. He would obey whatever directives they gave. Passing the buck was always a safer option.

The Final Briefing

The Uighur trio and interpreter Hieu arrived in the laboratory under cover of darkness, and were received by the two nuclear physicists and taken down to the basement. There, Abduweli, Yusup, and Ehmet – all still disguised as Chinese fishermen – were introduced to the single bomb made by the scientists with radio-active device in it. They were instructed on how to release the safety catch and set it off by remote control or by setting a timer. They were then shown the five IED bombs with the implanted radio-active devices that came all the way from Bulgaria. A detailed description on the after effects of the detonations was given to them. By now the trio had their eyes almost popping out of their sockets.

"This is big!" exclaimed an elated Abduweli, "Bigger than what we have been trained to handle, and decidedly more effective. But, ….yes … we can handle it".

"Where are we going to use it?" enquired Ehmet and got a look of disapproval for interrupting the Professor – the older looking of the two. He got no answer.

The scientists next took them to an adjoining room that appeared to be some sort of dressing room with a shower bathing space. They were given one set each of radioactive protective gear; ochre colored overalls, a bluish-grey cloth cap to cover the hair, a yellow helmet to wear over the cloth skull-cap, a radiac measuring instrument slipped through a red ribbon to be worn around the neck, white cloth covered shoes with rubber soles, and white gloves with 'RCA' written prominently on it in English in red paint. They were also given face masks with filters.

"You will be required to wear this during your final assault," said the Professor through the interpreter.

"Now, we are expecting someone to come to brief you on the final assault. He should be here within the next hour" said the senior of the two scientists as he looked at his watch. He stared at the three relatively 'uneducated Chinese fishermen' intently, and wondered whether they would be able to carry it off, and whether all that they had done was worth the effort.

They lingered around for awhile, with very little conversation through interpreter Hieu. There was the tension of expectations in the air. While waiting, each of those present had their own individual thoughts going through their minds.

The junior scientist was mentally going through all the procedures that went into making the bombs to cross-check that nothing was missed and that a hundred percent success would be guaranteed provided the arming and detonation was done properly.

Yusuf was living through all the training they had been through at various places to convince him that there was nothing more to be learnt.

Ehmet's thoughts were in far away Xinjiang, the place that would celebrate with joy when they had completed their task.

Abduweli was mentally working out the distances they had travelled to arrive at this moment, and was wondering whether an easier and shorter way could not have been found?

Hieu was waiting for all this to be over so that he could go back to Vung Tau, situated at the mouth of the Saigon river delta, from where he was plucked out and brought here to perform this role.

After what seemed like a long wait, there was some noise upstairs, and the Professor went up to escort no one less than the ubiquitous Hafiz down, who on entering immediately loudly proclaimed,

"I would like to be left alone with these three Chinese fishermen please, laying stress on the word 'Chinese'. I speak Chinese, and so will not require an interpreter." He pretended not to recognize the trio and would not look them in the eyes. The four of them were led to an adjoining room. All this was done with great speed. After locking the room from inside, he scanned for any cameras fitted in the room, placing a finger over his lips, signaling them to keep quiet. On finding the coast clear, he hugged each one of them tightly, and kissed them on both cheeks.

"Allah has been great! He has safely led you through all your travels and training and brought you to this stage to commence your final phase and avenge the death of our fathers, mothers, sisters, and brethren who died at the hands of the Chinese government. They are continuing to kill our people even to this day. I have no doubt that Allah will help you in delivering a sledge hammer blow on the despicable Chinese" said Hafiz.

He quickly asked them to tell him all that had happened since he had last met them. They, on their part, were overjoyed to see him, and like excited school children went through all that had happened. A few questions and counter questions followed and they were ready for the next part.

"Now listen to me very carefully," said Hafiz. "Your target is the nuclear power plant on the island of Hainan, in Tangxing Village of Haiwei Township in Changjiang County." He pulled out a map of the Gulf of Tonkin and Hainan Island as he was saying this. As Chinese fishermen, you will take the Chinese trawler out under cover of darkness and stay clear of all fishing during daylight hours, but engage in innocent fishing whenever anything is sighted. It is about two hundred nautical miles to your destination from Haiphong. The GPS onboard your trawler has the arrival coordinates already set in it. You have to follow it and arrive at your destination under cover of darkness. There is a westerly wind blowing these days. You will detonate your bombs in the nuclear power plant and the winds will blow the radioactive particles downwind across the island. Oh! I forgot. Before you disembark from the trawler, change into the overalls and equipment they have given you in this lab. That is the gear the Chinese power plant persons wear. It will give you that split second advantage you will need to get out of a sticky situation, should you be confronted by any of them or the security personnel. You also have sufficient arms and ammunition onboard for a successful onslaught and withdrawal"

"Have they given you the gear?" He asked and they nodded by way of confirmation.

He continued, "Use the night-vision equipment and the blinding laser guns to advantage, without any hesitation. Now come around me and look at the map, and layout of the nuclear power plant."

Hafiz then ran through the entire operation with them four times; once with each of them separately till they got it right, and then with all three together. He gave them possible situations of Chinese boats earlier on, and shore security personnel later on, confronting them, and in clinical professional fashion told them how to deal with them. He explained the terrain in detail to them as if he had been there himself. But, in reality, he had got this information from 'Google Earth' and the Chinese internet *Baidu*. He handed over drawings, maps, and other essentials to them.

"Now, this is not a *jihadi* operation. It is a *fidayeen* operation. Remember! Once the explosions are set off, all the instruments worn by the power plant operators will show dangerous radiation readings, and they will be more concerned about saving themselves than anything else. The winds will take the radioactive particles across the island and cause mass hysteria and eventual evacuation. You have to wear your face masks and withdraw under cover of darkness, get as far away upwind as possible from that coastline, and then slow down at first light and act as normal fishermen till you get to Vietnamese waters. I am giving you a satellite phone linked to someone in Turkey. Use it only after you have carried out your attack, while in the withdrawal mode. That someone will be expecting your call. He will then give you orders on how to get back to Turkey." He handed over the phone to Abduweli. He also handed over some Chinese currency to each one of them separately – no more than what an average fisherman was expected to have.

"Make sure you load some fish onboard before you leave these shores, to make it appear as if you had caught them. Lastly, I want each one of you to write your Wills and give it to me. It will be useful should you, by any chance, not be able to get back. It will be torn up in front of you when you return." The three of them looked confused but complied.

"Any questions - anyone? Remember, after we open the door and step out to join the others, I will not be talking to you any further. May Allah be with you! Remember, this is what you had been waiting for, all these months. This is what you have trained for, all these months. This is what you have covered large distances for, all these months. I have full confidence in you. I know you will succeed. That is why I picked you for this task." The conversation ended. He hugged and kissed each one of them one final last time. They opened the door and stepped out with expressionless faces. The trio picked up the bombs and clothing equipment and they filed out of the room, up the stairs and out into a waiting van. Hieu accompanied them. Hafiz stayed back and waved out to them. He then returned inside the building with the scientists. The assault team, driven by Hieu, headed for the seized Chinese fishing boat.

Black Panther

The Gulf of Tonkin was peppered with competitive fishing activity harvesting marine products that formed a vital part of the diet of both the Vietnamese and the Chinese common man. But unknown to these fishermen, beneath the same busy waters lurked a black, all-steel behemoth, tracking them, and watching their every movement. It had the ability to track hundreds of them simultaneously. With her stealth characteristics, she was almost undetectable. Inside her hull, sixty two men toiled hard like a well-oiled machine to ensure she functioned as she was supposed to, for the task she was allotted. The current sortie of hers was for three months, and she was permitted to freely patrol within the confines of the South China Sea to perform her role.

Captain Sharma had just returned to his cabin after a work-out in the gym. He did this regularly and ensured that the whole crew did their work-out on a regular basis. The gym was not a luxurious one; it was extremely small and cramped, and one that would not attract anyone in an urban city with its uninviting looks and restricted space. Yet it was a vital part of the Black Panther, for her crew. The long, arduous, months at sea in cramped environs did not make for healthy living. Exercising was vital to keep mind and body alert. The gym had been specially designed with equipment that was noiseless and with no loose objects around that could be accidently dropped by a careless individual.

This was the third patrol the Black Panther was on in the South China Sea with the present Captain. It was a busy sea with hordes of merchant traffic and many warships and submarines of littoral nations milling around, carrying out naval tasks for their respective navies. The Black Panther was an 'outsider', but she was there to offset the invasion by the Chinese navy into the Indian Ocean, and to gather information about this newly rising force that was upsetting the balance that had prevailed in both waters for centuries. The Chinese naval base, with futuristic plans to support a very large navy, had come up in Yulin, on the island of Hainan. Strategically, it was an ideal location and well chosen. It gave control over the South China Sea, and easy access to the Indian Ocean. Ships and submarines were already operating from there, but in small numbers for the present. The Black Panther was watching these movements keenly.

Captain Sharma had a wash and settled down to routine work. A glance at his electronic display at the foot of his bed showed that all was well in the Control Room. He flipped the pages to check on the machinery spaces and the Reactor Compartment, and found all was 'okay'. Then he turned his attention to the Torpedo Compartment and the Missile Compartment and found everything in order. He just about got into his bunk with a book to relax when he heard an intermittent buzz coming from his Command and Control Unit in his cabin, accompanied by an orange flashing strobe light. The Unit was nicknamed "Knocker" by submariners as signals and messages from the gadget generally spelt 'excitement'. He tensed up and called his Second-in-Command to his cabin immediately, ordering him to bring his key to the unit. Both the Captain and the Second-in-Command had to insert their keys to open the Command and Control Unit. One individual could not do it by himself with one key. Soon there was a knock on the door.

"Come in, Arun, and shut the door behind you. Have you brought the key with you?" he asked in a reverential tone.

"Yes Sir! But what is the matter?" enquired the Second-in-Command of his Captain. Silently Captain Sharma pointed at the "Knocker". The buzzing had stopped, but the strobe light was still functioning.

"Good Heavens, Sir!" reacted Arun, with excitement in his voice. "Did it also buzz?" The Captain nodded. Then he continued, "Shall we open it?"

"Why do you think I asked you to come with the key?" snorted the Captain. They were both on edge now.

They followed the laid down procedure, a highly classified one that only Commanding Officers and Second-in-Command Officers of nuclear submarines knew. Just before sailing out on a sortie, they would be given a change in code settings every time. After a complex set of procedures, the final decrypted message came in.

"Deliver two pregnant rabbits to Papa Romeo by midnight. Await further orders. Acknowledge."

Both of them stared at what they had just read, for a long time. 'Rabbits' meant the Remotely Operated Underwater Vehicles they were carrying onboard; 'pregnant' meant they were to be armed; 'Papa Romeo' was the code for a position at the approaches to Yulin Harbor. Both were wondering what was afoot. There was tension in the air. They went about preparing the acknowledgement which was also an equally complex procedure that took a good two minutes. That done, both headed for the Control Room.

Captain Sharma looked up at the chronometer and then at the Command Display in front of him. Operating a few switches and buttons, the touch screen, and a ball marker, he satisfied himself that he had enough time to get to a safe position from where he could release the ROUVs so that they get to their assigned position in time. The ROUVs that they had onboard could be remotely operated silently from the submarine up to a reasonable distance away, and propelled to even greater distances. They carried explosives that could be remotely detonated by the submarine when required. They could also be used as a prowler in a chosen area to gather recorded information, and recovered after the assignment. They could lie on the bottom of the sea bed and gather information, or move as ordered by the handling operator, and collect data on the move. In a calm voice the Captain of Black Panther ordered a change in course, and the behemoth responded with alacrity and settled on its new course. The Captain did not want to announce anything to the crew as yet, and so he sent word for the Weapons Officer to come and see him. The Weapons Officer was responsible for the Missiles, Torpedoes, and launch, recovery, and operation of the ROUVs of which there were four onboard.

"Vijay, get two armed ROUVs ready for launch. Get your team going and report when ready. I shall tell you when to launch them," said Captain Sharma in almost a whisper so that others in the compartment would not hear him. He then showed him the launch position and the destination on his screen. "I shall transfer this data to your screen so that you know what to do," the Captain continued.

"Aye, aye, Sir!" whispered the Weapons Officer and left the Control Room. He did not question his Captain. Everything onboard the submarine was disseminated on a need-to-know basis. If no reasons were given, then no reasons were sought. That was it. The relationship between the Captain and his Second-in-Command was, however, very different. They shared everything.

"What do you think is happening, Sir?" enquired Arun of the Captain in a whisper so that others in the compartment could not hear.

"I haven't the faintest idea. We shall wait and see," responded the Captain.

Captain Sharma was right. He wasn't to know that a certain Jimmy Ahuja was behind this message he had just received. Only a few days earlier, the R&AW Chief had had a meeting with the Chief of Strategic Defense Forces who directly controlled all Strategic Forces. He controlled the Black Panther too. His organization came directly under the Prime Minister's Office and acted independent of the Army, the Navy, and the Air Force headquarters. Taking him along, Jimmy had met the Prime Minister and the National Security Advisor and they were cooped up in the Prime Minister's office for a couple of hours. The two of them had then returned to the Office of the

Chief of Defense Forces for another lengthy meeting. This was the outcome of all that – or at least the beginnings of something to follow.

The Captain ordered the Second-in-Command to bring the Black Panther to 'ultra quiet state'. A series of orders and actions followed. The Black Panther silently crept her way towards the approaches to Yulin naval base, avoiding the moored Chinese underwater detection sensors that she had located and plotted during her many earlier sorties to the South China Sea. She was at her silent best, and when in this state, she was among the quietest submarine in the world. There were some noisy small craft on surface, moving around in the area, but none of any concern. They were being watched carefully on the Sonar Screen. These craft were not on any specific patrol in defense of the harbor and were probably supply-vessels shuttling between Yulin and the reef islands the Chinese had armed and manned.

The Weapons Officer reported that he was ready to launch two armed ROUVs, and had a third one standby in case one of the selected two malfunctioned. Captain Sharma nodded in approval. The Weapons Officer, Lieutenant Commander Arun Fadnavis, was excellent in his work and an above average officer. Indeed, the entire crew was above average, and had been specially selected for service onboard nuclear submarines after proving themselves onboard conventional diesel-electric boats.

At the appropriate time, the two ROUVs were released. They were released from a special chamber in the submarine that could be flooded and drained for launch and recovery of these small craft. They silently sped away to their destination with the Weapons Officer remotely operating them under direct supervision of the Second-in-Command. On reaching position Papa Romeo, they were made to rest at the bottom of the sea. Two self-destruct 'decoys' were released in altogether different directions and away from Yulin naval base, to keep watchful eyes and ears busy. The decoys would emit unfamiliar noise patterns that would confuse listening ears and keep them engrossed and busy for awhile. The Black Panther withdrew seawards in an altogether different direction to a safe position, but within range of the crafts she had just released. The Captain withdrew to his cabin with a million thoughts going through his mind, rehearsing mentally for any and all possible contingencies that may arise as a result of this maneuver. He stared at the 'Knocker', almost willing it to come alive again so that the suspense would end, but it remained inert. He cursed and lay down in his bunk with his book, anticipating many hours of sleeplessness ahead.

Gulf of Tonkin

After the session with Hafiz Mohammed in the late hours of the night, the trio was driven to the fishing vessel with their latest and prized acquisitions from the lab. On getting to the pier, Hieu had stopped short of the boat and bid them farewell, wearing a broad grin with his yellow buck-toothed teeth visible in the dim light of the early morning sky. He disappeared into the darkness with the vehicle that had brought them. That was around 4:00 am. On the make-shift pier Hoang and Dat had been waiting with huge plastic containers of fuel for the boat. They helped the trio embark them and to top up their fuel tanks, returning the empty containers back to the pier. There was more than enough fuel to take them up to and back from Hainan, about 200 nautical miles away. At the end of fuelling, they still had some extra unopened containers. "Stow them away forward of the Steering House. That will be close enough to the replenishing point", ordered Abduweli. The fresh water containers embarked the previous day had been stowed in similar fashion next to the fresh water replenishing point. In an hour's time they were done with the fuelling. Dat and Hoang shook their hands and disappeared down the country road. The Uighur, disguised as Chinese fishermen, remained below decks with one on 'Watch' in the enclosed Steering House from where the boat and its engines were handled. They needed to rest, and be wide awake and alert once they arrived at their destination. There was the unfamiliar smell of fish that permeated throughout the boat which the three land-lubbers from the central Province of Xingjian found detestable. But it had to be endured. There was some fresh fish onboard as part of the deception plan.

Dawn was just about to break as Abduweli, Yusup, and Ehmet slipped the ropes from its moorings, started the engine, and quietly moved the fishing vessel out of the isolated bay, into the wide open Gulf of Tonkin. It was a Friday, August morning. They had faced Mecca and said their prayers on deck before casting off. It was an incongruous sight for anyone to behold – three Chinese fishermen saying their *namaaz*! Luckily, no one was around. It was going to be a hot day. Temperatures in the Gulf of Tonkin this time of the year hovered around 40 degrees Celsius at noon. A gentle westerly breeze would be their only reprieve, but coming from the starboard quarter and following them, it would hardly be effective. Humidity was also high, and for those not used to the sea – like this trio – the journey was going to be an uncomfortable one. As luck would have it, there were no other boats in the vicinity. The vessel settled down to a very gentle roll with the muffled staccato beat of the engines barely audible in a largely quiet morning. Ehmet was first on the steering wheel. The practice sessions they had were apparently not adequate, and it took some moments of unsteady weaving before he could reasonably steady the boat on the course indicated by the Global Positioning System (GPS).

Yusup was below deck, getting some arms and ammunition out for the three of them in the dimly lit cabin and reflecting on all that had happened in the last twenty four hours. Abduweli knew that they had to move beyond five nautical miles from the coast as quickly as possible, to avoid the coastal fishing crowd of Vietnam that provided the country with over eighty percent of the nation's marine catch. The fishing boats were expected to put out to sea any time now. That coastal belt, which falls inside the 30 meters sounding line, is infested with small and medium sized fishing boats by the hundreds all day. In deeper waters, the density of boats dwindles. Then there is a void, and beyond that the larger Chinese trawlers exploit the Gulf of Tonkin from Hainan and the mainland. The occasional boat that strayed into the Chinese fishing area invariably got rammed and sunk by Coast Guard vessels. Abduweli was advised by Hoang and Dat, through interpreter Hieu, to stay on the outer periphery, and out of hailing distance, from the Chinese trawlers by day. They were to close the coast of Hainan only towards the latter half of the day, towards nightfall - or earlier if there were no boats or other craft around. He was also below decks, with Yusup, in the confined space of the trawler, rearranging the weapons and ammunition, and gingerly stowing away the bombs they had got from the lab.

The arduous training, the indoctrination, the many classroom sessions in different languages, and the thousands of miles they had traversed this past year had transformed each one of the trio from a largely peaceful-minded but agitated soul belonging to Central Asia, into hardened, steely-nerved commando-like fighters, ready to be deployed anywhere in the world. With adrenalin freely flowing through the body and with total dedication to the purpose at hand, there were few who could be expected to match them in their newly acquired prowess. The genesis of all this hatred for the Chinese as a race had taken seed very early in their lives when they saw and lived through the countless massacres and inhuman treatment they had witnessed their tribe being subjected to, including the loss of their loved ones back home in Xinjiang. This had been going on for years, and was still happening. The thirst for revenge was an undying one that they nurtured inside their hearts like glowing embers that could never be doused. In fact, aided and abetted by their mentors throughout the training period and during their travels, they were now totally committed to do their worst, and even give up their lives, if need be.

While sharing a meal together, Ehmet broke silence first; "Do you think we can pull it off?"

The other two had their mouths full and so were quiet for awhile. Then Yusuf spoke, "What do you think? Why are we in this boat after all these months and months of training and travelling, if we are going to fail?"

"I am beginning to get butterflies in my stomach, and the reasons are unknown to me," continued Ehmet.

"What can go wrong?" countered Yusuf.

"Why! A number of things can go wrong. We may not reach; the boat can sink. Someone can attack us from another ship – a Chinese one. The engines may pack up and we may drift till we run out of food. The Chinese may be on to us and may be waiting for us to reach their coast to finish us off. All that will be left of us then will be the Wills we wrote and handed over. From the moment that was asked for, I began to get butterflies in my stomach. Why did he ask us to write a Will? Is he not expecting us to get back?"

"Shut up! – Both of you! We have been trained to be *fidayeens*." barked Abduweli. "You do everything as per instructions, backed by the training we have gone through, and there will be no reason for us to fail. We will do the job and get back to Istanbul. Of that I am sure," he ended.

Trawlers are meant to fish at slow speeds. They were not equipped for fast transits. Their engines were powerful, but the gear ratios of the gear box were designed to haul in heavy, fish-filled nets at slow speeds, without tearing them. It was just as well. Moving about at high speeds in these waters would make them noticeable. An hour out, and they were well clear of the Vietnamese coastal fishing belt that extended up to five nautical miles from their shores. Another hour later, there was no land to be seen anywhere. To the landlubbers, this was upsetting. At the speed at which the trawler was moving it would take them the whole day, the night, and the whole of the next day before they get anywhere near the coast of Hainan. Aided by the currents of the Red River flowing into the Gulf, they should arrive off Tangxing Village of Haiwei Township, in Changjiang County, just after sunset on the following day, which was perfect provided all goes well. Yusup and Abduweli rigged up the boat to put out its fishing gear at short notice the way they were shown during training. They would lower it if the presence of any vessel was observed. They then retired below deck for some rest. Every three hours, one of them would relieve the helmsman in the wheel-house.

By a strange coincidence, the Gulf of Tonkin had a visiting navy at the same time. As a part of its demonstration of operational reach, and new 'Look and Act East' policy, a part of the Eastern Fleet of the Indian Navy was exercising with ships of the Vietnam Navy over a period of one week. The Indian Flotilla, led by Rear Admiral Ghorpade, was on its way back from visiting Vladivostok (Russia), Pusan (South Korea), Sasebo (Japan), and Subic Bay (Philippines). After these exercises with the Vietnamese Navy, they would be visiting Port Kelang (Malaysia) and Singapore before returning to their base on India's Eastern Coast, having been away for about three months. The usual 'attack and defend' games that naval forces play at sea was being exercised, with the Vietnamese frigates, corvettes, missile boats and one Kilo Class submarine from the First and Second Regional Commands defending their coastline, while the Indian Navy with their stealth guided missile frigates, corvettes, supported by a Fleet Tanker, were acting as the attacking force. The Black Panther was around but not talked about as it was operating independently.

While on his constitutional walk in Lodhi Gardens in New Delhi on Friday, Jimmy Ahuja received a message from Bangkok to say that the trawler had sailed out of Haiphong a few hours earlier. He could hardly suppress his glee. The frustration of not being able to share this bit of news with anyone was something he just had to endure. He decided he would visit the satellite tracking station to get them to track a lonely Chinese trawler heading from Haiphong towards Dongfang City on the west coast of the Island of Hainan.

He was also aware that the Indian Navy had its presence in the same waters at that time. Then there was the Black Panther. Jimmy had taken a long shot and convinced higher authorities to let her have a role to play. He was lucky to get their approval and cooperation.

The Approach

A new day dawned. It was the first Saturday of the week, in the month of August. The previous day had been a long and arduous one at sea, but a lucky day for the trio. There was very little fishing activity in the middle of the Gulf of Tonkin, and the first trawler they sighted was well after midday, heading south. By then they had covered some one hundred and ninety nautical miles from their start point.

There was one worrying factor though; not far away from them, and between their boat and the coastline of China, was an oil tanker painted in the color of a warship, moving up and down in a north/south line. Through his powerful binoculars, Abduweli observed that it was not flying the Chinese flag but a white flag with a red cross on it that he did not recognize. On their first night, the tanker had moved across to south-westward of them and disappeared over the horizon. Yet with first light, they saw it back on their eastern side. It showed no apparent interest in their boat and stayed well clear, and on the horizon. The trio decided they would keep a watchful eye on the tanker while discounting it as a threat.

Onboard the oil tanker, however, everyone on watch on the bridge were aware of the presence of this lone Chinese fishing vessel making its way diagonally across the Gulf of Tonkin. The orders for the Indian ships stated that they were to keep an eye on any or all Chinese warships, aircraft, coast guard ships, and fishing boats in their area of exercise during idle moments of exercising with the Vietnamese Navy, without closing them or raising any suspicion of interest. It was in their exercise orders in the section marked as 'Intelligence'.

While Yusuf was handling the vessel during his Watch, a Chinese maritime reconnaissance aircraft circled around the oil tanker for awhile, and then flew over their fishing boat. It headed in a northwesterly direction and disappeared into the distance. They did not see it again.

Not to be left out of the excitement, during Ehmet's turn in the bridge, he suddenly saw a moving thick vertical spar – only a spar – make its way down the starboard side of their vessel. It appeared to be made of steel and seemed to be looking at them, or at least rotating, because the sunlight flashed off it occasionally. What was it? The trio could not figure out. They were not to know that it was a submarine periscope. It showed itself briefly and then lowered itself and disappeared. A sense of uneasiness prevailed after this sighting that slowly wore off with the passage of time.

The time was now around 4:00pm. The trio sighted four Chinese trawlers together on the southern horizon. They definitely did not want them to close their vessel. Yusuf immediately steered his vessel away on an easterly course till the trawlers disappeared from sight. He altered the boat back to point towards the spot they were to arrive at, guided by their GPS, keeping between seven to ten miles from the west coast of Hainan. This way no one could noticeably see the trawler from landward and neither could the trio see the low lying coastline from where they were. Now that the coast was clear, they hauled in their fishing gear that they had turned out earlier to the 'standby' position. The requirement to lower it never arose since they had not encountered anyone at close quarters. They then pulled out their weapons and fired a couple of rounds into the sea at some chow cans they had tossed overboard, with each one taking the wheel while the other two honed their skills. These weapons were with silencers and coughed when fired. They did not make noticeable noise. By sunset they were close enough to see land on their port bow and ahead, which only confirmed that they were on the right track. They said their *namaaz* and prepared for the big task before them. At twilight all three of them changed into the rig given to them back in the lab in Haiphong, to look like workers in the Changjiang

Nuclear Power Plant. They discarded their smelly fishermen's clothing and piled them in one corner of the cabin below. After the operation, they would be required to wear them again till rescued. They retained their Chinese disguise, and strapped on ammunition under the coat and armed themselves to the hilt. The remotely operated bombs were also brought up on deck. Abduweli took one light one and the heaviest one; Yusuf and Ehmet took two light ones apiece. The remote control's batteries had all been charged. It only remained for them to activate the circuits on each of the bombs and set it off with a push of a button when ready. The bombs were wired in such a way that one signal from the remote could set all six of them off, and any one of them could press the button as they had a remote each. This was dangerous but a necessary one, as they were explained during the briefing. The trio pored over the maps supplied by Hafiz one last time and memorized details, then rolled them into balls and threw them overboard. All lights in the trawler were then put off.

By the time they reached their destination, just a little north of Haiwei harbor, it was completely dark. They cut the engines, quietly lowered the anchor, and waited awhile for a reaction from ashore. Peering from cover, they studied the land carefully under the diffused light that was prevalent. They could see the narrow strip of white sandy beach before them, and the faint darker outline of the dense growth of casuarinas trees beyond. This was good. The trees would provide them some cover. Behind the trees, and over the tops, was a light glow from the power plant lighting beyond. They could barely make out the two breakwaters jutting prominently out to sea. The road leading up to them from the Nuclear Power Plant was not visible, but that did not matter. They were not about to go to the breakwaters and make their way down the road. They were going to hit the casuarinas grove south of the breakwaters, in a 'line abreast' formation, and move through it to the point where it ended, before breaking out in the open. Mentally, the trio was now tuned to the mission at hand and did not think of anything else. Each one went over the drill they had been taught in Pakistani camps and the tasks they had assigned amongst themselves tonight. They had already gone through it thrice at sea, after sailing out from Vietnam. They even went through a Plan 'B', should Plan 'A' fail. They were reasonably confident of achieving the tasks set out before them. The adrenal was now flowing freely. There was no discernible movement on the beach or around that they could make out through their night vision goggles.

Gingerly, and careful not to make any noise, they lowered their light small skiff which they had with them. They boarded it and silently rowed ashore. Once they beached, they quickly lifted the skiff out of water, and took it into the casuarinas grove ahead. It was not an easy task. All of them were fully laden with ordnance and weapons. The skiff appeared to be a bit heavy, which in fact it wasn't. It took a few moments for them to catch their breaths. They hid it in the bowers beneath the casuarinas and rested awhile. Then Abduweli gave a hand signal and they moved in line abreast, ten feet apart, across the grove till they came to its edge. There they assembled together again.

Peering ahead, they found a clearing in front of them, about 80 meters deep, that ended along a path running parallel to their casuarinas grove and at right angles to their line of sight. Across that path was another flat open space with some shrubs interspersed here and there. That ran about another 20 meters deep. Beyond that space was a high boundary wall of the Plant with a proper road running all along it, on the outer side. The lights of the campus behind the wall were throwing up a glow which made it easier for the trio to look around and spot things. To the right of the casuarinas grove were salt pans. Between the salt pans and the casuarinas grove, was a narrow path that appeared to be joining up with the road along the boundary wall. It also cut across the parallel path ahead of them, at right angles. To the left of them was another road, a broader one that appeared to be leading from the breakwaters to join up with the boundary wall road. It was a bituminous road that was probably made to take heavy loads. There was no sign of life, but there was a tall sentry post behind the wall, overlooking the road leading up to the breakwaters. If there was a sentry there, he was not visible. Ehmet tapped the shoulders of the other two and pointed to the left of the sentry post and to the base of the wall. In the dim light they spotted a gate at the end of the road. Strangely, it was not lit, but it was closed. They were briefed by Hafiz that the main entrance was on the landward side. This gate was used whenever stores had to be transferred from the jetty to the power plant.

The three of them got into a huddle and discussed the situation in whispers. There must be one, possibly two sentries up there in that watch tower. They would have to be taken out. Yusuf was the best shot of the three and pulled out the CS-LR3 – 5.8x42mm sniper rifle slung on his shoulder. Abduweli and Ehmet pulled out their hand-held blinding laser guns from their shoulders. All three weapons were fitted with telescopic sights. On a signal from Abduweli, the three of them sprinted across the clearing in zigzag fashion, crossed the road, and took positions behind shrubs. In their white clothes, this was a big risk they took, but a calculated one, since it was dark. Taking aim in the direction of the sentry box, Abduweli made a loud animal-like noise. They were right. Not one but two heads popped up from the sentry post in the watch tower and began peering in the dark.

Two well directed laser guns immobilized them and simultaneously, "Phut! Phut!" Yusuf pumped two bullets into the hapless sentries. They dropped in their tower silently. Dead! A quick look around to see all was clear, and the three of them ran up to the wall and crouched against it, two of them back to back, running their eyes in opposite directions long the top of the wall, and the third one scanning the roads. All was quiet. This maneuver had gone off well. The next assault was going to be on the gate.

Abduweli pondered over the next step. For the assault on the gate, a different plan of action would have to be executed. They could approach it from the road in bold fashion with darkness behind them and diffused light from the power complex ahead of them. The advantage would be theirs but somewhat negated by the white clothes they were wearing. It would be better for them to creep up to it along the wall to reduce the chances of detection and reaction time for the gate keepers. They would have to be quick as they had already killed two sentries, and it would be a matter of time before they were discovered. Time was of essence, and the trio just had to get into the Power Plant complex quickly and disappear among the many buildings inside. Abduweli signaled the plan by code to them, using one of the sign languages they had been taught in Waziristan. The other two nodded in acknowledgement.

The Dragon Snorts

Yang Zhen, the Head of Counter Intelligence was an astute man in his early forties who had risen to his present position through sheer dint of performance. From humble beginnings – he was the son of a farmer in the Pudong belt of China across the Huangpu River from Shanghai – he benefitted from his father's sudden acquisition of wealth to get a good education, and later a good post in the Intelligence Department. His father's plot in the farmlands off Shanghai was acquired in 1992 by the government to set up a Special Economic Zone that was opened up to the whole world to come and invest, or to set up industries in. His father got a handsome monetary compensation by Chinese standards, and an apartment across the river along with other rehabilitated farmers. These farmers, including his father, were then coerced to change over from farming to being employed in the many industries springing up in the Pudong New Area. Yang Zen and his siblings went to better schools where all of them performed well. Yang Zhen got admission in Shanghai University of Political Science and Law, where he excelled. He joined the Intelligence Department and soon was admired for his acumen and sharp perceptive talent to anticipate and often accurately forecast incidents.

As the Head of the Counter Intelligence Bureau, Yang Zhen had been kept very busy when the threat to Guangzhou had been announced, and for many weeks thereafter. Now, the Head of Domestic Affairs Bureau had come in with the news that another threat was imminent, and this time from seaward. As usual, the input was inadequate and vague, and that was most frustrating. China had a very long coastline. He studied the problem in its entirety with all the earlier available information, and his instincts led him onto narrowing the threat from China's vast coastline to a narrow area. He decided to meet his boss and put forward his theory.

When he entered Xin Sheng Zong's office, he found him in a not too pleasant mood. That was alright said Yang Zhen to himself because he seldom found him in a good mood. Perhaps it was the pressure of being in that chair he thought to himself. On the other hand, it could be due to his impending retirement. He walked up to the desk and waited to be told to sit before he settled into the lush leather padded chair in front of the Minister for State Security.

"Have you come to give me more problems?" growled the Minister as he stared at him over the half reading glasses poised at the end of his pug nose.

"Sir, it is about this intelligence information we have just received about a threat to our coast-line from seaward," began Yang Zhen. He continued, "We have no inkling of where on the coastline, and our coast line is very long. So I embarked on an exercise to see if I could narrow it down."

"Have the attackers taken you into their confidence?" asked the Minister sarcastically.

Yang decided to ignore the remark and continued, "You see, Sir, I looked at the state of affairs along our coast line before this information came in. There is stability with our neighbors along the coast, everywhere. Taiwan is presently quiet, and so are South Korea and Japan. We are having skirmishes only in the South China Sea. The Gulf of Tonkin is also relatively peaceful ever since our government and the Vietnamese government agreed on the demarcation of the Gulf for sharing fishing rights." He paused, looking at the Minister for a reaction.

"Go on" said the Minister. He was listening.

"I then asked myself, how would I, as an attacker, come to attack from seaward? One way would be to come with an armed group, but that would be suicidal and probably doomed to failure even before any landing takes place, given our defense set up along our coast. It would be better for me to come in as a tourist. Then I looked at the areas of interest that was drawing the attention of the world at large, in recent times. Sanya City has been in the news and is being talked about avidly in the media in many parts of the world. Sanya City is open to tourism and we have many tourists coming there throughout the year. Of course we scan them all properly, and keep an eye on each and every one of them from the moment they arrive till the moment they leave. But that is where I would come if I was the attacker, and my target would be the large number of tourists in the city. I could come as a tourist by air, land in Haikou airport, and take the ring railway like any other normal tourist to Sanya City," said Yang Zhen.

"Impossible!" snorted the Minister. "You think we opened Sanya City to the world for tourism without considering this possibility? I am surprised to hear this from the Head of Counter Intelligence Bureau. You of all people should know how that is next to impossible."

"Yet, *not* impossible, Sir!" he interrupted, and then remained silent for a brief moment for effect, all the while watching his superior. He continued, "I have learnt never to ignore what seems impossible as not possible. However, there is one other possibility I have considered. We have recently permitted cruise ships from other parts of the world to visit Sanya City. They come only for a day. Thousands of tourists are disgorged by the ship for a couple of hours. An attacker or attackers could come as a tourist or tourists on a cruise ship."

The Minister was now looking worried. He did not like the idea of his Bureau Head persisting with targeting Sanya City. Yet, He realized that he was talking some sense. Cruise ships? He had a point there.

"So you think the target is Sanya City in Hainan?" asked the Minister.

"I think it is the most likely place that an attacker would target in today's conditions. However, an attack on nearby Yulin can also not be ruled out, despite it being well guarded by the navy" replied Yang Zhen, carefully choosing his words.

"And who would this attacker or attackers, be? Which country would they come from? Eh?" asked the Minister with a hint of sarcasm back in his voice.

"I think they would be hired agents, Sir. And it would be done with every trick in their books being used to conceal their true identities. The 'Filipinos', for example, could be the initiators. But I think that is unlikely as the 'Filipinos' are not quite up to it. At this stage I am only looking at quelling an attack and not at who the initiators are. Perhaps people more senior than I could look into those aspects," replied Yang Zhen.

"Alright then! Pass the orders down the line as coming from me that all border and coastal forces are to be on high alert till further orders. The island of Hainan is to be reinforced with extra forces in and around Haikou, the airport, Sanya City, and the circular rail stations, and inform the PLA (N) to boost up their security around Yulin naval base" said the Minister with an air of finality.

He dismissed Yang Zhen, who withdrew with a satisfied gleam in his eyes.

The Alert

Chinese Coast Guard patrol boat No 86001, while patrolling between Dongfeng and Xinzhou on the western sea face of Hainan, noticed a small contact on its radar that appeared not to be moving. It was close to the shore, just a little north of Haiwei harbor. The Patrol Boat belonged to the 1st Border Defense Coast Guard Detachment (*zhidui*) at Haikou, and would not have been normally patrolling these waters. There were three such Detachments on the Island of Hainan, with one each in Haikou, Sanya, and Wenchang. Having received recent orders to increase vigilance against a possible terrorist attack from seaward, the three detachment commanders had been ordered to extend their patrol areas to cover the entire perimeter of the island. The Haikou detachment was given the west coast of Hainan to patrol, and that was how the patrol vessel found itself in these not too familiar waters.

On approaching the static radar contact, Patrol Boat No 86001 found it to be a Chinese fishing vessel anchored in very shallow waters. The Commanding Officer assumed it was in some sort of trouble as Chinese crews generally over exploit their vessels, and suffer frequent breakdowns. Since it was dark and there was not enough depth of water, the Commanding Officer hailed the fishing vessel through a megaphone, but got no response. He tried again ....and again ....and again for the fourth time. That was strange indeed! He decided to lower a skiff with a few armed sailors to board the vessel and inspect it. This evolution took awhile. The men in the skiff boarded the fishing vessel and saw no one onboard. There was a catch of fish that did not look too fresh. There were enough signs to show that men had been living onboard not so long ago. Three sets of smelly clothes were also found in the cabin below. The vessel's papers were found in the wheel-house and appeared to be in order. There were no untoward signs of anything unusual that could give rise to suspicion, except for the fact that no one was onboard. The armed sailors made their report to their ship over a megaphone. The Captain of the Patrol Craft asked them to return. The Chinese Patrol Craft resumed her patrolling of the coast and headed northwards, making a signal to its Detachment Headquarters in Haikou about the abandoned, anchored, fishing vessel.

It was a Saturday evening, and all the shore establishments were manned by their duty staff, with all the top officers enjoying a peaceful week-end. Some of them were even beyond reach till Monday morning. The daily signal traffic moved slowly. The signal made by Patrol Boat No 86001 went through routine channels without any urgency, and drew attention only around 2300h.

It drew the attention of Yang Zhen, the Head of Counter Intelligence, while he was going through signals of interest. Sixth sense told him that the fishing boat may not be as innocent as it looked. He opened his laptop to study a map of the area. Suddenly his knees buckled. The fishing boat was anchored just off the Changjiang Nuclear Power Plant! And there was no one onboard the vessel! That only meant that they had stepped ashore. Now, why would an innocent fishing vessel anchor off a beach for the crew to step ashore, when it could very well enter Haiwei harbor? – Or a jetty somewhere? – Or a pier? Yang Zhen sprang for his telephone and rang up a series of people, one after the other.

His first call was to the Head of the Nuclear Power Plant in Changjiang County, who lived in the campus along with other members of his vast team. He was asleep. Yang Zhen woke him up and screamed impatiently like a man possessed, "This is Yang Zhen, Head of Counter Intelligence, speaking from Beijing. Your plant is under threat of an attack. The attackers have come from seaward, and may even now be inside your plant. Get every man and woman who is breathing out of their beds and to their stations. You don't have time. Hurry up! Catch the attackers and there will be suitable rewards."

His next call was to the 1st Border Defense Coast Guard Detachment at Haikou. He directed them to return the patrol boat back to where they had sighted the fishing vessel and to guard it, killing anyone trying to board it, or anyone who was already onboard. If the fishing vessel had weighed anchor and left, it was to be located, pursued, and captured.

He called up his Counter Intelligence teams on Hainan Island and gave them instructions. He called up other authorities in Haikou, and in Sanya City, taking care not to call up anyone too senior, whose feathers could be ruffled, to the detriment of his career. Things could be managed at his level. It may turn out to be a damp squib. It could also turn out to be real. If it was going to be a damp squib, he could always say that he had carried out an exercise at his level. If it turned out to be the real thing, he could justify that he was quick off the block, and reap the benefits to follow.

The Director of the Nuclear Power Plant got out of bed and made a few calls. The siren for general alarm was to be set off, and the actions to follow were to be carried out as written in their contingency plans for such an eventuality. He began to dress up to go to the office – his office. All these years he had been dreading the possibility of a nuclear accident but not of a terrorist attack. Now here it was, on his plant, under his care! Even as he was on his way to the office, the siren went off, sounding the alert. He could see his security forces in vehicles tearing down the roads in various directions. Good! Things were happening fast, he thought to himself with a sense of satisfaction.

Going for the Jugular

One hundred and fifty meters below the sea, out of the way of the shipping lanes and south east of the island of Hainan, the Black Panther was on patrol; prowling around and waiting; listening and searching, in accordance with the requirements for which she was deployed in the South China Sea. Inside, her hull was a beehive of activities. Her orders were explicit. The Commanding Officer had the freedom to move as he chose, where ever he chose, and whenever he chose, with one overriding factor - that she must not be detected, or her mission compromised, at any time.

Amidst his normal busy schedule onboard, Captain Sharma glanced towards the calendar on his desk and saw that it was a Friday, - the first Friday of the month of August. They had been on patrol for a month now. It was by no means over. Underwater, one lost all sense of day and night, and days of the week. It normally did not matter. There was no sunrise or sunset to see and admire. That privilege went to conventional diesel electric submarines that lurked around periscope depth every second or third night to ventilate the boat and charge batteries before going deep for the next few days. Even onboard those submarines, only those on Periscope Watch had the privilege of peeping at the outside world. Nuclear propulsion boats very rarely came up to periscope depth. They did not need to.

Captain Sharma was pensive. The Indian warships must have returned home after their exercises with the Vietnamese navy. His submarine had not been asked to join them. He would probably have been there, if the aircraft carrier was operating, but she was not a part of this Task Group. He had tracked and followed them from the Taiwan Strait to the Gulf of Tonkin and then withdrawn. This was just to see if they were tailed by any Chinese submarine. He had not detected any. He glanced at the 'Knocker'. After launching those two ROUVs, no further instructions had come. They had been accurately positioned at 'Papa Romeo' which happened to be at the entrance to Yulin harbor. They must be picking up and recording all activities there. He was not aware of what he was to do next; retrieve them with recorded data? Or, … what? He had been ordered to launch them in an armed state. Since launching them, he had hung around the south eastern approaches to the Chinese naval harbor, at a safe distance away from the moored sensors, yet within range of communications with his launched vehicles. Since he had not been briefed about this deployment of the remotely operated vehicles before sailing, he would have to wait for the instructions that were expected to follow. In the wardroom - the officer's mess - there were some discussions soon after Weapons Officer, Vijay, had 'leaked out' that he had launched two of them. There were low murmurs for some time till one of the officers picked up courage to find out.

"Sir, why have we launched our 'remotes'?" asked the junior navigator across the dining table while having a meal.

Captain Sharma frankly related everything that happened, which wasn't much. The crewmen who launched the remotes must also have spread the word after the launch, in the crew's quarters. The Captain, however, chose not to take the crew into confidence and announce anything on the main broadcast at this stage. A sixth sense told him to hold back. In any case, the next course of action was not known. He dismissed his thoughts and turned his mind away to other present matters.

Unknown to Captain Sharma, back home in New Delhi, Jimmy Ahuja had been in discussions with the Chief of Strategic Defense Forces, giving him intelligence inputs, and working out the next course of action between them. The 'Chinese' trawler was on its way, and was being constantly tracked by the Indian satellite above; the armed ROUVs were in position and the Black Panther was awaiting orders. The timing for the next course of action had to be just right. One other staff officer, sworn into secrecy, was working with the two of them to feed them with inputs to arrive at a decision.

Friday night passed and Saturday arrived. Inside the Black Panther's hull, the 'Knocker' broke its long silence and began sounding its intermittent buzzer, flashing its strobe light at the same time. The Captain looked at his watch. It was 6:00 am local time. He quickly sent for his Executive Officer, the Second –in- Command. It took Arun awhile to come as he was at that moment pooping in the Heads (the WC). When he finally arrived with the key, the two of them got down to following the laid down procedure to get at the incoming message. After decryption, there it was finally, in plain language. The Captain stared at it, reading it very carefully, with Arun peering over his shoulders doing much the same.

"At midnight on the night of coming Saturday/Sunday, send your rabbits to the warren. They are to litter there. The delivery should end successfully before 2:00 am. Return undetected to handler post-haste. Acknowledge."

They both looked at each other, trying to assimilate what they had read, and went back to reading the message once again. The Second-in-Command was the first to speak.

"Have I got it right, Sir? They want us to direct our two ROUVs to the entrance of the underground submarine pens and explode them between midnight and 2:00 am. Thereafter, we are to high-tail it back to our base in the Nicobar Islands?"

"I am afraid so, Arun. Obviously something is going on back home that has forced the hand of the Chief of Strategic Defense Forces to execute this order. I wonder if CPEC has caused more problems, or if this is in retaliation to that last incident? Or have there been problems elsewhere on the border?" The Captain brooded and went on, "Quite obviously this is a low intensity reaction, and by calling us back they are not expecting it to escalate. In addition, they probably want to make it as difficult as possible for the Chinese to nail it on our boat, and our government, and leave them guessing. That is why they probably want us out of the area pronto. We have time in hand. We have the whole day before us."

Arun nodded his head in agreement and went on, "Shall we get on with preparing our acknowledgement, Sir? Then we can get the navigator to get us closer, and Vijay to take over controls of the rabbits and prepare for his midwife duties." He smirked, quite pleased with his choice of words. They both got down to sending their acknowledgement through the 'Knocker'.

The Chief of Strategic Defense Staff received the 'acknowledgement' and conveyed the same to a very anxious Jimmy who was sitting beside him in their Operations Room. On getting the message Jimmy's pulse rate surged, and the adrenalin began to flow. He could hardly hide his excitement. Months and months of homework, planning, preparation, and execution had gone into this. It simply must not fail, said Jimmy to himself.

The Black Panther steered a westerly course till the mouth of Yulin harbor was on her starboard beam at some distance. The Captain brought the crew to the highest degree of alertness and readiness. Torpedoes and decoys were brought to instant ready use if required. They may land up in a situation where they might have to use them in self defense. Then he gave the order:

"Weapons Officer, execute your task, to completion, as briefed"

"Aye, Aye, Sir!" came the acknowledgement through the headset.

Thereafter, Vijay's trained mind and hands got working on the controls. First he raised one of the two 'remotes' from the sea bed where it was resting. Anticipating a boom (wire net screen) positioned by the Chinese at the entrance, to prevent unauthorized entry into the naval harbor, he made it hug the bottom of the channel and glide through its central portion where the water would be deepest. The 'remote' was sending him visuals and the visibility was not bad at all. It took him an hour of careful handling, at creep speed, to get it in position.

"First one positioned. Taking the second one across now" reported Vijay to the Captain.

He got down to shepherding the second one to join the first. Strangely, it took longer as movement of harbor craft in the vicinity degraded his control signals to the 'remote'. He had to wait till things settled down before moving it further. After two and a half hours, both were in position and he reported completion of the task to his superior.

Captain Sharma looked at his watch. It was showing 23:31h. Excellent! Everything was set half an hour before schedule. The Black Panther slowly and quietly reversed course and was now heading due east. Deeper waters lay ahead of her now. When the harbor entrance came on her port beam in another half hour, Captain Sharma decided he would start the rabbits' labor pains and quick delivery.

The Assault

Slinging his weapons out of sight behind him, and with the pistol covered in his hand, Abduweli stepped out and walked normally along the wall and up to the gate. When in front of it, he let out an audible low wail and crumpled on the ground facing the gate and lay almost still on his left side. He pretended to be clutching his stomach but that was only to hide the pistol in his hand. He moved one leg jerkily to show he was alive. He however was alert and peering at the gate. The gate opened and three men ran out to him, shouting in Mandarin. They never reached him. Six noiseless shots brought them to the ground, two from Abduweli's pistol and four from the sniper rifles fired by the other two. All weapons that were fired had silencers. Ehmet and Yusuf ran up to Abduweli and helped him drag the three bodies to the far side of the gate and laid them out along the wall. One quick look to ascertain they were all dead and the three of them walked through the gate and shut it from inside. They hid in the shadows of the gate and peered inside. They were inside the Changjiang Nuclear Power Plant!

They could see the domes of the Reactor Containment buildings to their left, higher than the other buildings around them. Keeping their weapons concealed, they walked along the left side of the road from the gate at a quick pace, in the shade of three buildings on their left. They came to an intersecting road. They crossed over and continued down the original main road till they came to two long buildings on their left. Not a soul was in sight anywhere. They turned left, into the gap between these long buildings and found themselves facing the Reactor Containment buildings right ahead, about eighty meters from them. They paused in the shadows of the longer building as some movement was noticed near one of the Containment structures.

Two men, similarly attired as them, had just emerged, and were heading in their general direction. They hadn't noticed the trio. They were engaged in some intense conversation. Yusuf had his sniper rifle out while the other two had taken out their stun guns. As the two men were about to be fired upon, they turned left and disappeared down the road, away from the trio. They were lucky – for the moment. The trio held their fire. Five down so far! They needed to get to the Containment buildings to place their bombs and quickly withdraw out of range, without drawing too much attention. There was no further movement in the vicinity of the Reactors and the three of them split as planned and headed for three of the four Reactor Containment buildings in front of them.

Abduweli, who had two bombs in the pack on his back, made his way to the center of the three chosen Reactors Containment buildings. Ehmet and Yusuf, carrying two smaller bombs each, headed for the Containment structures on either side. They had been told that it would be virtually impossible to enter the Reactor Containment buildings. Those buildings housed the Reactor Vessels, the Pressurizers, and the Steam Generators. The buildings were all made of very thick concrete walls, and were always manned. Two pipelines were expected to come out from each of the Containment buildings. One would be high and out of reach. The out-of-reach pipe-lines would be the steam pipe lines leading into the adjacent buildings housing the Steam Turbines. After turning the turbines, the spent steam would be led into Condensers where they would condense to water. This water would be led through return pipes, at a lower level, back into the Containment buildings. These return lines could be easily reached, and they had been instructed to attach their bombs to these return pipelines and withdraw. The trio had gone over the drawings and layout again and again on the trawler and memorized it before throwing the paper overboard. They were quite aware that, with the safety arrangements in place in this and all such nuclear plants all over the world, the bombs would not be harming the main Reactor systems per se. They would only be rupturing the return pipeline, resulting in draining out the water from the system, and causing severe damage to other buildings and installations in the vicinity. The damage would be substantial, but the exploded bombs would also be releasing radioactive particles in the air. That would, expectedly, create a massive human reaction, and result in panic and evacuation of the islanders, which was their intention. They succeeded in attaching the bombs to the pipe lines, and retreated to the space between the two long buildings they had first emerged from. It was decided that they would set off the bombs by remote control once they had reached near the main gate.

As they retraced their steps towards the gate, a loud siren pierced through the peace and tranquility of the place, and continued non-stop, endlessly. The startled trio began to run for the gate. They could see a lot of people emerging from various buildings. They were all running helter-skelter and therefore their own movements at first seemed in sync with the general scene. They had just reached the last three buildings, now on their right, when they heard a vehicle at some distance behind them that seemed to be coming their way.

"Now press your buttons! May Allah avenge the death of our Uighur countrymen" shouted Abduweli to Ehmet and Yusuf in their language. All three pressed their buttons on the remote control simultaneously, on the run. They reached for their anti radiation masks and put them on.

As the Director of the Plant entered his office, he heard deafening explosions coming from the direction of the turbine and generator rooms of the power plant. There was a gush of hot air that entered, along with smashed pieces of glass from his office window that scattered all over the flooring. A few pieces lodged on his face and neck and he began bleeding. Within moments his radiac measuring gadget on his person began clicking continuously, showing dangerous levels.

"My God!" he muttered. This was it! Holding a kerchief to his face, he made some calls and directed his staff to execute the emergency shutdown drill and commence evacuation of the area. Pulling his anti radiation gear out of his cupboard, he quickly put it on and ran out of his office.

The general alert was initially promulgated through the loud siren which would have got everyone to report for duty to their place of work. After the explosions, it was followed by a different siren sound that all personnel dreaded and were familiar with. It signaled the order for shut down and evacuation. There was pandemonium in the campus. The Director tried to contact the Containment Reactor building but lines were down. He hoped there would not be a melt-down as he drove off in his car, to pick up his family from his house, and leave the premises. On the way he glanced towards the Containment buildings and he thought he saw bodies lying on the ground, and some being dragged away by survivors. There was fire and heavy smoke rising up to the skies and blowing away towards the east. There was debris everywhere for a thousand meters or so from the center of the explosions. He did not wish to delay getting away and so did not stop.

The Withdrawal

A security officer in a vehicle saw three men in white apparel running towards the side gate leading to the sea front. He thought they were heading for the gate to augment its staff. Suddenly the blood froze in his veins, as he observed that they were armed. What were slung over their shoulders could only be weapons. They also had masks on. They were dressed like staff members, but only his security men carried weapons. Through the loudspeaker on the vehicles cabin top he asked them to halt. At that very moment there were loud explosions heard from the direction of the Reactor Containment building, followed by all round blasts in ripples. The three men who were running towards the main gate swung around and began to open fire on the vehicle. The security officer returned fire from inside the vehicle, while directing the driver to weave aggressively. Another vehicle joined him from behind and also began firing. The three men on the road split and went in three different directions, with one of them continuing to make a dash for the gate. He came under a hail of bullets and went down. The other two managed to take shelter behind two buildings on either side of the road. As the vehicles came within range the surviving two threw grenades on them. One missed the target, and the other got the second vehicle, which blew up with bodies thrown out of it in pieces.

The vehicle explosion drew two more vehicles in the vicinity to the spot. They also had armed personnel inside. The lead vehicle shouted instructions in Mandarin over the loudspeaker to the other two vehicles to the effect that there were two armed men on either side of the road, hiding behind buildings, and they were to be eliminated. All three vehicles stopped and the men inside tumbled out and split into two groups – one moving to the left and the other moving to the right. Another grenade landed and exploded, decapitating a few more of the security men.

Abduweli realized that it was now difficult to get away. Ehmet had bought it and from the corner of his eye he saw him fall on the road while he, Abduweli, was dashing for cover towards the building on the right. He presumed Yusuf was still alive in the building across the road from him. The withdrawal had not gone well. He had thought for a moment that they would get away and reach the casuarinas grove before anyone gave chase. A diversion needed to be created, for any hopes of getting away. That opportunity presented itself in the next few seconds.

Another siren – of a different type – suddenly blew continuously. Everyone in the Nuclear power plant dropped whatever they were doing and headed for the main gates, some running, some in vehicles, and some in two-wheelers. Obviously this was a general evacuation of the place. A mass exodus had begun.

Abduweli, removing his mask and taking advantage of the dark, joined the crowd and ran out of the gate. So did Yusuf. Separately, they both branched off at a suitable time and opportunity, and went into the casuarinas grove where they met up just short of the skiff they had tucked away. That was the drill they had worked out – to get back individually, should they be separated, and meet at the place they had stowed the skiff in. They would wait till all three reached, pick up the skiff, launch it, get to the fishing vessel, weigh anchor, and head out to sea. They both knew that Ehmet would not make it as both of them had seen him go down. They hugged and clung to each other for a moment to let the tension drain out. They had just carried out a very dangerous and seemingly impossible task for which they had prepared for months and months. Both were grinning from ear to ear with glee. "Come on! Let us pick up the skiff and get to our boat" said Yusuf and they both ran for the skiff.

A fire had started inside the power plant and they could see black smoke rising up to the sky and blowing away from them, landward.

Donning their masks, they lifted the skiff and broke out of the trees, heading for the fishing vessel. "There it is! Hurry! Hurry!" said Abduweli, and they began to run with the skiff in their hands. They did not know that the boat had been discovered. They did not know that a general alert had been sounded about their boat. They did not expect anyone to be there waiting for them.

They were greeted by a hail of bullets from both sides. The skiff fell to the ground. Yusuf's skull split and he went spinning to one side and lay very still. Abduweli was spun around by a host of bullets from all sides that riddled his body, and he hit the sandy beach, writhing in agony. He looked down at his body and saw blood spurting out of his chest and stomach. Soon he was finding it difficult to breath. He tried to raise his weapon to return fire but found he lacked the strength. He could not spot anyone either. Gradually his mind and his sight went hazy. He was fighting to keep his wits about him, but began to lose consciousness. He shut his eyes as he gasped for air heavily through his mouth.

He saw a vision of himself as a little boy hiding behind a refuse bin across the road from his house, watching his mother and his siblings being mowed down in a hail of bullets by Chinese Han authorities. They were screaming one moment and then went silent abruptly. Tears were rolling down his baby cheeks but not a sound was coming out of his mouth. He was crouched and rooted to the spot.

A hand suddenly lifted him up from where he was squatting behind the bin. He looked up to see the figure of his smiling mother reaching out for his hand. He stretched his small hand and grasped hers. She began pulling him up. She was floating in the air like an angel. She was lifting him and taking him up higher and higher, away from the ground. Down below, he could see his body, now that of a little boy crouching behind the trash can, now that of a big man lying sprawled on the beach, growing smaller and smaller. His vision blurred and slowly went blank till all he could see was a brilliant white light all around, accompanied by a strange calm.

Soldiers in Coast Guard uniforms emerged from the casuarinas grove and picked up their bodies and loaded them into a vehicle. They drove off at a fast pace, away from the Nuclear Power Plant. Hoards of people, with terror and panic written all over their faces were running down the roads, heading north and south. Some were crying; some were carrying bundles; some were carrying children. None of the vehicles on the roads, stopped for any of them. It was a case of survival. There was no time or room for humanitarian deeds.

Elsewhere, on the island of Hainan, in Yulin, at the entrance to the tunnel sheltering submarines, two loud underwater explosions rent the silence of the night with plumes of water rising up hundreds of feet in the air. Even as naval personnel in the vicinity and ships' duty staff saw it, tremors were felt on land. They saw the entrance to the tunnel caving in, and the hillside above it sliding down like an avalanche from snow-topped mountains. The tunnel was not visible anymore. Then there was a momentary silence. A few minutes later, sirens and hooters went off everywhere as pandemonium and a host of activities followed.

At some distance outside the harbor, and many meters below the surface of the sea, a black behemoth silently slipped away, gradually increasing speed and depth to maximum to make her way out of the place – homeward bound.

The Aftermath

The nuclear reactors were rendered safe, as shut down drills were quickly carried out. But there were high levels of radioactive particles in the air that swept over the Island of Hainan from west to east, carried by a strong breeze. Geiger counters in every nook and corner of the Nuclear Power Plant had chattered noisily, showing radioactivity above danger levels, which initiated the process of evacuation of the entire Nuclear Power Plant.

The Island Administration announced a general evacuation of the island that turned out to be a major evolution and a nightmare, as the westerly winds steadily blew across the whole of Hainan, carrying radioactive particles with it. There was no knowing how far and where all the contamination had spread. The contents of those six bombs were not suspected at first. They had to err on the positive side as a safety precaution, and presume the leak was from their Nuclear Power Station. Such an eventuality had never been rehearsed. Total mayhem and confusion followed. It would take time to complete the process of evacuation.

Evacuations began in Sanya City also, even while the Chinese navy went on full alert. The stations on the ring main and the trains were getting filled up; there were many cars on the roads; the airport in Haikou was getting more and more crowded by the hour. This unprecedented mass movement was getting difficult for the authorities to manage. On the flip side, naval personnel were combing the beaches and coastline; road blocks were being enforced; people were being searched, making movements that much more difficult. All types of marine craft that were present began to head out to sea, towards the mainland. Naval ships sailed out to execute searches for an unknown assailant.

The media was quick to announce about the explosions and the action being taken to evacuate the personnel, but they had no news as yet of the state of the Nuclear Reactors. A lot of discussions and speculation followed. Not a word was mentioned about the explosions in Yulin naval base.

Twenty four hours later, Beijing officially announced that the explosions were caused by three Uighur terrorists who had come by sea in a Chinese trawler, disguised as Chinese fishermen. It was suspected that they had set off 'dirty bombs'. How many bombs and how powerful, was yet to be ascertained. All three had been shot dead. There was some damage in the Plant, but the Reactors were safe. All four Reactors had been shut down to carry out a detailed inspection. No mention was made of how many personnel in the Plant had lost their lives. An evacuation of all persons from Hainan had been ordered, as it was necessary. The population was ordered to refrain from eating fruits and vegetables harvested from the island, or drink the local water. They would be rehabilitated on the mainland and put through medical checks. The affected would be given prompt treatment. Beijing also announced that it would take time to render the island safe and only after that would the residents and tourists be allowed to return to it.

The Chinese government accused the Vietnamese government of aiding and abetting the terrorists. Vietnam strongly objected to such accusations and stated that the only trawler they had captured from the Chinese some time back, had been stolen by unidentified Chinese miscreants a few weeks earlier and taken away, out of Vietnam waters. They even had photographs of the three Chinese fishermen onboard, sailing away with the fishing vessel. They accused the Chinese government of orchestrating that move.

Ships from the naval base at Yulin, after sailing out with their pre-wetting systems on, were relocated elsewhere. The fate of the submarines inside their hillside shelter, if any, was not disclosed or commented upon by the Chinese government.

The media all over the world highlighted the incident. Tourists were advised not to head for Sanya City. 'Acts of Terrorism' were condemned by many. The United States and India, among others, expressed sympathy and deplored the incident.

Jimmy had not gone for his daily walk as it was a Sunday. On Sundays he took time off from his Lodhi Gardens trips. Early that morning he was told that 'it' had happened. He opened the newspaper to see if the newspapers had got to it. The news of an attack on the Nuclear Power Plant on Hainan Island and its evacuation was on the bottom of the front page. He read it out to his wife over breakfast while poring over the paper.

"Who could be responsible for this?" She asked him.

"They say Uighur separatists; three of them. All three have been killed. They were only the executors. The real persons who orchestrated the operation will never be found" he said with a smirk. With a pleased look, he finished his breakfast and put away the paper. Just before noon, there was a call from No 10, Race Course Road, asking him to come over. Jimmy drove into the Prime Minister's residence. He was expected and escorted in.

"Ahuja *sahib*, have you read today's newspaper or seen the TV News?" asked the Prime Minister.

"Yes Sir! I have. These terrorist are getting bolder and bolder. We can expect Beijing also to condemn acts of terrorism hereafter, Sir," replied Jimmy with a straight face. Did he see a look of admiration in the Prime Minister's eyes, or was it just his imagination running riot?

"What, in your opinion, will the after-effects of this be?" enquired the Prime Minister.

"Well, Sir, they are assuming that the island has been polluted by radioactive particles, and are in the process of evacuating the whole island. It will be isolated for some length of time and then they will have to localize the infected areas and clean up the whole place, including their fresh water lakes that they use for drinking, and their tilled land, before they can start bringing people back, Sir. Tourism on the island is going to be hit badly, and that will affect their economy in the region; agricultural activities on the island will come to a halt.

It has come at a bad time for the Chinese, Sir. There may be other repercussions also. The Hague decision in favor of Philippines is not accepted by China and has put her in an uncomfortable position. She may try and sow seeds of discord and disharmony among the ASEAN by selectively tempting some of them with generous aid and loans on easy terms to get them on her side and reduce threats. Pressure on neighboring fishing vessels and warships in the South China Sea may be stepped up over the next few months under the guise of curtailing terrorist activities. However, we should continue with our naval presence there as a visual support to the littorals there. The newly elected President of the United States must be secretly happy with the state of affairs in the region, Sir."

Nothing more was said, and Jimmy left the PM's residence a little disappointed, though he knew full well that he could not be publically or privately rewarded. Someday….. Someday, thought Jimmy to himself, he would have a story to tell.

A day later, the gizmos he had received from Langley suddenly went dead, and could not be revived. Jimmy destroyed them.

Two days later, Jimmy attended a reception in the British High Commission and ran into Al Turner, the CIA agent from the US Embassy.

"The Chinese are quite upset about the Uighur attack on their island and even more upset about their reach" said Turner, searchingly.

"They took on the Uighur in Xinjiang unnecessarily. Now it is payback time. Pakistan can be congratulated for having trained them well" said Jimmy, and he winked at Al Turner and moved away.

Far away, in Istanbul, Hafiz Mohammed silently mourned the death of his dear friends, the trio, who had struck a heavy blow on behalf of the Uighur on the Chinese government. He had grown fond of those three dedicated and fully committed men from his clan. The attack had been successful. The Chinese were wincing and hurting after the blow. He shed a few tears for the trio, and then gathered himself. He would now get down to planning the next strike.

Chinese naval activity in the Indian Ocean hit an all-time low across the next two years. Captain Sharma was honored with a medal by the President of India with a vague citation. His name was in the list of awardees announced on India's Republic Day. So was the name of the Captain of the Strategic Deterrence submarine (SSGN), that of the Captain of the aircraft carrier, and that of a Commanding Officer of a conventional submarine, among others.

Epilogue

Terrorism and terrorist organizations the world over, are here to stay. They will continue to be a thorn in many nations' sides for years to come. Waging 'war' in this form is the cheapest way dissidents, rebel organizations, and weaker nations can draw the attention of the world to their appeals, needs, and claims, however justified they may or may not be. They could, and will, join sides in pursuit of their overlapping or common goals. They will kill innocent citizens, politicians, military personnel, government personnel, children, and also create untold damage to property. They are ready to die in the process. They do not care. There are many examples of this all around us today.

Terrorism is decried everywhere as the bane of peaceful and progressive societies, and something that must be eliminated. In a world where nation state dominance, influence, maneuvering and positioning is an ongoing phenomenon, terrorist organizations clandestinely provide them one of many persuasive tools that can be exploited to advantage as yet another means to an end. The story here provides one such example. There are countries already using terrorist organizations through their national intelligence set-ups for carrying out their wars against other nations. This is an open secret, known to all nations.

The tools used by dissidents, separatists, and terrorist organizations are increasingly becoming more and more sophisticated. From ever increasing financial support, to more sophisticated recruiting and training, to use of better and better delivery systems and causing ever increasing damage, the bar is consistently being raised to higher and higher levels. Nuclear devices are weapons that terrorist organizations are all striving to get their hands on to exploit. It is only a matter of time before this becomes a reality. 'How to make a nuclear bomb in your backyard' is no longer a secret; the information is readily available in open literature and in the electronic media. There are many abandoned arsenals in and around Russia, after the break-up of the Soviet Union, that have fissile materials that can fall into wrong hands. Once they get their hands on these, they would soon have a choice between using 'dirty bombs' or actual nuclear heads to achieve their goals. 'Dirty bombs', while not so destructive, have a powerful psychological effect on the people in the vicinity. This has been explained briefly in one of the sections of this book. Of course there are always the other types of weapons of mass destruction as alternate options – biological, chemical, and those that climatologically cause catastrophes.

What of the South China Sea? Will China be able to run roughshod over world opinion and dominate and control the water space? There are reasons to believe that she will. Her determination to do so will see it through. At the moment of writing this book, she has already made overtures attractive enough to begin weaning the Philippines away from a long standing relationship with the US. She has coerced Vietnam into keeping a low profile. She will offer large sums of money and resources to other ASEAN nations to wean them away from western influence. She will farm the South China Sea resources and take the lion's share, and continue to handle minor skirmishes with her neighbors from a position of strength. The forces she has based on Hainan, and those deployed on shoals and reefs converted into little fortress islands, will ensure her dominance of the area. For sops, she will permit the 'Right of Passage' to international trade, but under close scrutiny and under her watchful eyes. Her intentions were discovered too late by the rest of the world to counter or stop her in time. But that's the way the Chinese function.

There are reasons to believe that India, with the help of Vietnam, is likely to cause some discomfort to China in the South China Sea, as a quid pro quo to the discomfort it is facing through increasing Chinese presence in its own neighborhood. This confrontation and posturing is likely to continue for some years to come.

One feels sorry for the Uighur community. In the face of heavy odds, they will have to accede to Chinese intentions and plans, and learn to live in Xinjiang as second class citizens. Their population will reduce, and Turkey will continue to harbor those who flee the region. Sporadic acts of violence through people like Hafiz Mohammed and his groups, portrayed in this book, may flare up now and again over the years, but their numbers will only dwindle in the Province, as a consequence. They will remain as the unsung heroes of a vanishing tribe.

Short write up on the Author

A former naval officer, Commodore P R Franklin took to writing in retired life, after serving for 36years in the Indian Navy. His first published works were short stories that found its way into the book titled "On All Fronts – Stories from the Armed Forces", released in 2006. Then, in 2010, the National Maritime Foundation, New Delhi, published his next book titled "Submarine Operation". Moving on to semi-fiction, but still with a nautical theme, his third book titled "Foxtrots of the Indian Navy" was published in 2015. This is his fourth book, his first pure fiction effort, but one in which he cannot avoid a nautical theme, as in his previous ones.

While in the Indian Navy, Commodore P R Franklin specialized in Submarine and Anti-submarine warfare. He was awarded the Vishisht Seva Medal in 1995 and the Ati Vishisht Seva Medal in 2001 by the President of India.

He and his wife, Joya, reside in Bangalore. His e-mail id is: jalvayufranklin1946@gmail.com